CW00828323

About the Author

Keith Bullock spent time living in Austria, Iceland and Denmark before majoring in European Studies and pursuing a career in educational management. He is now a full-time writer and lives with his French wife in Malvern.

The Anniversary Trip, one of the short stories in this edition, has also appeared as a film, under the title: *Second Honeymoon.* It was presented at the Cannes Film Festival, 2008.

Dedication

For my long-gone mum and dad, Lil and Jack, who will forever remind me of Christmas... And for my own wonderful family who make it feel like Christmas every day!

Keith Bullock

===================

**Twelve Christmas Crackers
&
A Boxing Day Treat**

Festive short stories to make you laugh and
cry, smile and sigh...

ACKNOWLEDGEMENTS

Many thanks to my daughter, Tanya and son, David for their dedicated readings, prompt feedback and innumerable suggestions for improvement over many months. Thanks to son in law, Darren for a brilliant cover design. My wife, Catherine provided an enviable eagle-eyed attention to detail and an ongoing constructive commentary and son, Marc gave unfailing encouragement during an exceptionally busy period of his life.

CONTENTS

Twelve Christmas Crackers

&
A Boxing Day Treat...

1

A Match made in Heaven

Albert was no great fan of his doctor and so, as was her wont, when the time came around for the flu jab, Delphine popped along to the surgery alone. December had swept in with a vengeance and no doubt, winter viruses would be close on its tail.

'Well, that's that done for another year,' she said brightly, as she hung back her coat in the hall.

'They can *stick* their needles – anywhere but in me! ' said Albert hooking a finger into his fourth can of Stella. He was pleased with his pun.

Now the Grim Reaper keeps a sharp eye open for complacency and when the first wave of flu swept in, he got to thinking that it was high time he paid Albert a visit. It came as a shock to Delphine of course, to wake up to Albert's cold, grey form. Such a waste of yesterday's ironing, she thought – and the sheets had been only on the bed a day... Nevertheless, forty years with a partner is no small thing and she came close to a tear or two, as she put on the *Swan Teasmade* and poured herself that revitalising first morning-cuppa.

Delphine was not one to sit around and mope and even before Albert's *rigor mortis* had properly set in, she found herself mulling over the possibility of finding a new partner. In all fairness, it *was* nearly

6

Christmas and the prospect of wrapping presents just to herself, or worse – using both hands to pull the wishbone and her Christmas cracker... well, it just didn't bear thinking about.

There was Albert's urgent disposal to arrange, but in terms of the immediate future, Delphine felt an overwhelming urge to discuss her straitened circumstances with Elsie, her dearest friend. One quick phone call and by eleven, the pair were installed comfortably in *Joe's Cafe*, opposite the Co-op Funeral Home.

'It shouldn't happen to anyone this close to Christmas,' commiserated Elsie, as she tongued the froth from her large Cappuccino and repeatedly inserted a finger into her jam and cream doughnut.

'That's my point,' replied Delphine. 'I just can't do *lonely widow*... it's not me, is it?'

If her best friend harboured any misgivings about the delicacy of the moment, she disguised them well.

'Trawl the Net,' she advised, knowingly. 'Find somebody new... I found my, Mitzi there last year, the choice in poodles was truly amazing.'

In spite of, Delphine's redoubtable resilience to the slings and arrows of personal misfortune, a tiny shadow of doubt ran the length of her features. A private acknowledgement perhaps, of her waning female predatory skills. For after all, since netting, Albert they had lain redundant and rusting those many years... and might not now be sufficiently honed for such a high tech challenge.

'I'm not sure I want to be foraging around in the digital ether,' she replied sniffily. 'Me and my Albert may not have said our marriage vows, but he courted me proper and we even had a church blessing.'

'You're out of date, Gal,' said Elsie. 'Everybody's at it now. You get exactly what you're looking for and if it's holy approval you want, you can find Him online too.'

'You can't mean... *God?*' said Delphine, incredulously.

'The Man Himself,' Elsie assured. 'I've seen the site: *Skype Him - Tune in. Turn on. Chill out...* that's what they say. Never done it myself mind, but then I've got my little Mitzi.'

'But it's ridiculous to think that God could help?'

'Don't be so sure. Arranged marriages over the Net, they're all the rage. Big business, large client base − no way that God would have wanted to stay on the outside.'

'Well I never!' said the astonished Delphine. 'But I'd need a new computer, my Albert was such a technophobe.'

'Are you C of E, or RC?'

`I've never thought about it, really. I think my people were Baptist.'

`Well there's a bonus! Probably no waiting time with that lot − I've heard the bigger denominations can sometimes queue for days.'

When they had said their goodbyes, Delphine made a beeline for the nearest electrical store. Albert's floral arrangements would just have to wait. By six that evening, she was unpacked, hooked up and ready to go. With trembling fingers, she typed *God* into Search and *New Man Wanted* into Refine Search. Sure enough, there was his Skype address! Busy as He must have been, God called back instantaneously and asked how He could be of assistance.

He certainly looked the part, long white beard, flowing hair, beautiful blue eyes... but having been a long-term agnostic, Delphine was in need of some reassurance.

`But how do I know it's really You?' she asked.

`Well, belief has to come into the equation somewhere, Delphine.'

`Tell me where You are then,' she demanded, impertinently.

`I'm out here in the ether, in cyber-space. Omnipresent, All-seeing and All-knowing.'

`But that's no proof really is it?' said Delphine, warming to the polemic. 'I've got to believe it's really *You*.'

`If there was proof, there would be no reason to believe... *Knowledge* and *Belief* are mutually exclusive.'

Such a clever answer, she thought – genuinely worthy of the Creator.

God was growing tired.

'I've had to resort to that argument ever since Doubting Thomas,' he told her. 'Now make up your mind, Delphine. It's Christmas next week – meaning the Lad's birthday is just around the corner – so I've a lot on. Are you in need of My help, or aren't you?'

There was no sudden *leap of faith,* but nonetheless, Delphine felt sufficiently persuaded to take the plunge.

`My partner's just passed away. Silly! – You must know that. It's hasty, I suppose, but I wanted to ask whether you could help me to find a new man?'

`A new man, you say?'

`Oh, I'm embarrassed now. I told my friend it wasn't an appropriate thing to ask.'

`On the contrary, the topic comes a close third to miracles for incurable diseases and demands for big Lottery wins.'

`So you *can* help? D'You think that You could do anything this side of Christmas?'

`You need a specific branch of the *Holy Highway Website,* it's called *Heavenly Intros at Cloud Nine.com.* Most days it's quite overloaded, that's why I've been obliged to put the business-end, so to speak, out to an agency.'

`An agency?' echoed Delphine, unable to disguise her disappointment.

'Needless to say, I'm behind it and therefore the agency is *infallible.*'

'And it finds new partners for people like me?'

'It most certainly does!'

`I'll get back to you,' said Delphine and quickly zapped the connection. She was pleased beyond words, of course, but in need of thinking time. God turned away to other things. He could have taken umbrage

10

over the abruptness of Delphine's departure, but in truth, there was nothing between Heaven and Earth that genuinely surprised Him.

'Go for it!' exclaimed Elsie, when they met again at *Joe's Cafe* to choose the order of poor Albert's funeral service. In her excitement, she over-dunked her doughnut and a large segment detached itself into her lap.

'It's the *infallibility* bit,' said Delphine, aware of the sudden imperative to make haste with the despatch of her own patisserie. 'Call me an old romantic, but there's part of me still, that believes Love should be down to good fortune and chance.'

'At our age, Darling there's a ticking clock. Can you really afford the luxury of *procrastination*?' (It was a word that, Elsie had recently picked up from Tuesday Scrabble).

As she wiped the mess from her skirt, she felt piqued to observe the speed at which Delphine's cake was disappearing. 'If you want part of it left to Love's Lottery, ask Him to give it His five best shots – and stick a pin in the shortlist,' she advised.

At that particular moment in time, Delphine was immune to all sarcasm – rather, the advice had the effect of firming her resolve. Fortified too, by the refreshments, she took her leave in a purposeful mood. Within minutes of returning home she was back online. *Heavenly Intros at Cloud Nine.com* opened to wedding bells and an impossibly attractive bridal pair dodging confetti and entering a coach and four. Not Delphine's cup of tea at all, but before she could hit *Delete*, a fresh-faced Cyber man appeared with a greeting.

`Hi Delphine. God mentioned that you might be getting back to us. You're ready to go ahead, then?'

He knew about her... It was both flattering and embarrassing. Delphine felt obliged to continue. `I'm looking for a partner,' she confided. `But to be honest, I was hoping for a degree of choice.'

'Did God not explain that the selection process will throw up an *infallible* match?' enquired Cyber Man.

'Well yes, I suppose He did.'

'If you reply to all questions openly and honestly, your transparency will be rewarded with the *perfect* match. With over nine billion clients on file, our sifting and screening processes will guarantee you a future partner to fulfil all of your intellectual, emotional, spiritual and romantic needs. Why would you want choice beyond that?' asked, Cyber Man.

Why indeed, thought Delphine. She felt a frisson of excitement akin to the first time that poor Albert had slipped an arm around her waist, in the Roxy cinema.

There followed an intensive and thorough inquisition. Every last detail of her family history, her lifestyle, her tastes in men, food, fashion and the Arts was pulled from file and passed to Profile Processing. Her background and education were laid bare. Expert systems interrogated her mercilessly and threw up endless blinds and double blinds that occasionally reduced her to tears. She was forced to examine, assess

12

and reassess every thought, opinion, assumption and premise that she had ever held on men, love and relationships. Cyber Man reappeared as she was nearing the end of her physical, psychological and emotional strength. He was reassuring. They were now in possession of sufficient information to deliver her the perfect partner. All would be revealed before lunchtime, next day.

Elsie was on the doorstep at the crack of dawn and positively brimming with curiosity. She waved a bag of four doughnuts, by way of an entrance fee and begged to be allowed to stay. Delphine made tea and they settled themselves down before the computer screen. As the morning wore on, their excitement grew. Elsie was careful not to dunk anymore doughnuts, for should an accident have occurred, she had no change of clothing and was not prepared to risk missing Cyber Man.

Delphine's thoughts turned idly to Albert (who had been removed discreetly from the house only that morning). They had been so happy... Would he have approved?

`I loved you, Albert Dawes,' she murmured into her fourth cup of coffee.

'He *would* have understood,' said Elsie, encouragingly. 'He's no-more... and everyone has the right to happiness, Delphine.'

Delphine quickly cast aside her doubts. 'Soon, I'll know the identity of my new life partner!' she exclaimed excitedly.

At noon precisely, Cyber Man appeared on screen to a fanfare of trumpets. 'Delphine, your perfect match has been found!' he announced, with a theatrical flourish. `I have no wish to *crow*, but I'm delighted to reveal that the compatibility quotient is an astounding ninety-nine percent! A relationship truly made in Heaven!'

'Oh thank you! Thank you!' exclaimed Delphine. The two women were unsure of what to do next, so they stood and clapped loudly. Further triumphal music followed as numerous Cupids with hearts and arrows bobbed in and out of a white mist.

`Delphine, meet the new man in your life!' proclaimed Cyber Man, as the screen slowly began to clear.

A familiar face appeared.

`Albert Dawes!' squawked Delphine. 'But, that's my Albert, you fool!'

'It's your-' began Cyber Man.

`It's my poor dead, *Albert,*' shrieked Delphine, before collapsing in tears upon the sofa.

The embarrassment all but overwhelmed Cyber Man's printed circuits and the screen went suddenly blank. An immediate review took place at *Heavenly Intros* and the *Cloud Nine* site remained firmly offline all over Christmas. God was abundantly displeased.

It turned out that at the back end of the website, *Recently Deceased* deletions to the *Global Eligible Unmarried Males File* had been running two days late owing to the world flu pandemic. Poor Albert was still listed under *"Live"* on *Pending Removals.* It was an unpardonable blip in Infallibility Codes of Practice from which, God has yet to recover.

As for Delphine, to Elsie's permanent disappointment, she followed her first instinct, cast aside her computer and fell back upon the random idiosyncrasies of Love's Lottery. She's happily settled now with Percy Whetstone, an assistant-undertaker at the Co-op.

2

The Reunion

Harold chose his moment carefully and sidled unobtrusively into the fringe of a largish group as they passed through the enormous automated doors of the Cavendish Shopping Centre. Once inside, he artfully side-stepped the two bored-looking security staff and headed for a tried and tested pitch outside the busy entrance to Boots. With a practiced hand, he delved into the copious pockets of his huge red overcoat and pulled out a large tin mug, ready-primed with a copper or two. He gave the mug a long slow shake and hoped that the sound would carry plaintively enough to tap into any surrounding seasonal goodwill.

     The warmth of the mall came as sweet relief from the biting, raw cold of the High Street. With luck he would manage to stay below radar until late-night closing time. His spirits rose as he nodded his thanks to the woman behind the first fifty-pence coin. Back at the "Sally" there would be soup and maybe a mince pie. If the tin mug continued to fill, there might be enough for a *wee drop* beneath the covers, after lights-out.

     Winter had bitten early and hard and had clamped firm in the run up to Christmas. He'd had cause to visit Oxfam to beg long-johns. The manageress had been a *hard-nose,* telling him that they were not *that* kind of a charity – all of the goods were for purchase only. What kind of charity was that then, he'd enquired – making folk pay for the stuff? Finally, she'd seen sense and handed over the pair he was now wearing. They were stiff and scratchy, probably ex-army, but the warmth was there, so that was fine. As for the big, red, quilted coat he was wearing, it had been the gift of a Birmingham Rag Market trader. "You can have it," the bloke had said. "It won't earn me a penny in that colour."

Black wellies and thick socks completed Harold's winter wardrobe. The boots had been taken directly from the feet of Blind Jim. The poor soul had passed on at the "Sally" in early December. As the saying goes: *every cloud has a silver lining.*

'Merry Christmas, Sir,' he murmured, as at long last, a second coin tinkled into the mug. Disappointing – it was all down to the time of the year: shoppers entering the store were blinkered, focussed entirely upon their present buying. The centre precinct would be a better bet, near the Christmas tree and the cafes. It was an exposed area, wide open to security cameras, but people would be more relaxed there. He pocketed the mug again and shuffled his way along the glitzy shopping lanes, deaf to the sounds of nearby carols.

As he came to a halt under the brightly decorated tree, his eyes almost popped from his head. It was the hop, skip and jump and the bouncy pigtails – *he'd have known her anywhere!* Now, she was pointing excitedly towards the surrounding presents beneath the

17

tree and pulling fervently at her mother's coat, eyes filled with wonder. Mummy clearly had other ideas, as firmly but gently, she steered the protesting infant towards the gaily-coloured stalls of the Christmas Fayre, on the far side of the square.

But, could it be Carolyn? Surely, his little Carri would be much older now, almost grown-up? – She certainly *looked* like Carri. He tried to figure it out. Thinking no longer came easy. No, not possible... Carri had died; that's what had started it all.

He had loved her. Oh, how he'd loved her! He loved her still... He had wanted more children. Gillian had not. He had been persuasive; *stupidly* persuasive. From the very first month of the new pregnancy she'd been adamant that she would never cope. "It's all your fault," she'd say, "I'll never manage – it's not going to happen."

Over at the Christmas Fayre, the little girl's mum had encountered a friend; they were talking animatedly. She'd failed to notice that Carri had slipped her grip. Now the little girl was wandering across to a glittering shop window filled with moving fairy lights. Gillian talked on. *It wasn't Gillian,* he reminded himself; it was just some lady chatting to a friend. And therefore, it couldn't be Carri, either, could it? – *His* Carri had died many years before, beneath her pillow on Christmas Eve. It was so confusing... He looked over again and spied Carri gazing in awe at the shop window.

...On that fateful Christmas Eve, he had crept into her room so full of excitement and anticipation, to fill her stocking. He had found her cold and still. A rustling sound had made him turn to see Gillian, with her swollen stomach, standing there wearing a glazed look. "It's all for the best,' she had repeated and repeated, and then she had smiled and patted her bump."I'll be fine, I can cope with the one – I did tell you."

He had cradled Carri until the paramedics arrived and had refused at first to give her up. And Gillian had kept on smiling and patting herself and telling him that it was all for the best, all for the best... He shuddered and shrank his neck further down into the big, red coat.

Now, the little girl was tracing her finger along the window ledges, straying further and further from her mummy. Her attention was centred upon the presents next to him beneath the tree. Gillian and her friend chattered on, oblivious to all around them.

He took out a grimy photograph from within the folds of his coat and gazed softly upon it. Carri smiled up at him, as she had done always in life. He was never without her. Late at night in the hostels when the last drunken ramblings had ceased, he whispered goodnight to her and closed his eyes upon her face; under tarpaulin on the pavements, he lit matches and bid her flickering image, sweet dreams. He kissed her gently now and returned her to his pocket.

The little girl was almost beside him. From time to time her gaze strayed away from the array of parcels, to take him in. Now, she was staring directly at him.

Was it possible? Had she guessed? On the other side of the precinct, her mother talked on and on.

...In the immediate aftermath, he had visited Gillian several times at the hospital. Inevitably, there had been a court case. She was found guilty of murder on the grounds of diminished responsibility. Murder, not manslaughter. It was there, in *Section 2 of the Homicide Act 1957*, as amended by the *Coroners and Justice Act 2009*. There was not much that he could remember these days, but *that* he would never forget. The jury had concluded that Gillian was suffering from: "an abnormality of mental functioning, grounded in a previously undiagnosed chronic depression". It had been a tragic cry for help and her mind had provided its own contorted logic.

He had buried his Carri. His public persona went through the motions with a certain level of controlled dignity, the husband in him experienced no compassion and the father screamed long into the night. When they moved Gillian, he sometimes forgot to visit. They told him that there had been further mental deterioration and that she was now under a long-term mental care order. At home, the rooms began to fill slowly with the debris of take-away meals, countless empty bottles and unopened mail. Through the fog he registered dimly that the pregnancy had been terminated. Later, someone from his firm dropped by... there had been a cheque and an awkward final handshake.

He missed Carri. Please God... he wanted her back.

A hand slipped into his and a small, shy voice asked, 'Are you Father Christmas?'

'No my darling, I'm not Father Christmas.'

'But you've got a big red coat and black boots and a straggly beard.'

'I'm sure that I'm your daddy.'

The little girl giggled at the huge joke. 'But you *are* Father Christmas really, aren't you, because you've got all of the presents?'

'No, really, really, I'm your daddy,' insisted Harold.

'You're *silly*!' said the little girl and then her eyes showed concern. 'Why are you crying? You're all dirty. Don't you have to wash when you're dirty? I have to wash when I'm dirty.'

He managed a smile. 'I'm not crying now, my love, look! I'm drying up all my tears.'

'Mummy said I could meet Father Christmas and I could have one of those presents.'

'But they're all *pretend*, my darling.' He picked up a box and shook it. 'They're all just empty boxes.' Carri looked so disappointed that he thought his heart was about to burst. 'But there's a big toy shop just along the arcade,' he added. 'Perhaps Mummy will take you there?'

'Please, can *you* take me? Mummy's just talking and talking and talking with her friend.' The warm hand squeezed his own.

It was true, Mummy was still talking – Gillian had always been able to rabbit, rabbit, rabbit... The shop was close by, it would take only a minute or two. His heart filled with joy.

'Come on then, my little Carri, let's go and see those toys.'

'My name's Gemma, Silly Billy!' she said, giggling once more.

Harold smiled at her foolishness.

The toy shop was heaving with Christmas bargain hunters. Gemma stayed outside whilst Harold entered and squeezed himself between the toys and the shop window. There was no mistaking which of the dolls Carri wanted, she stood and pointed at it enthusiastically through the glass. Harold gathered it up and pushed it surreptitiously beneath the red folds of his coat. No one had noticed. He walked away slowly and calmly, to rejoin his Carri outside.

They began to stroll together along the palisade and Gemma jumped around excitedly at Harold's side. Her eyes were firmly fixed upon the huge bulge in his overcoat.

'Oh, please... *please* can I have it now?' she begged and finally, with a flourish, he revealed the doll and placed it into her outstretched arms. As Carri hugged it to herself and looked up at him with shining eyes, Harold felt that he had never been happier.

'You *really, really are* Father Christmas, aren't you?' insisted Gemma.

'I'm your daddy, Carri,' he replied.

Gemma giggled loudly. 'You're a Jolly Joker!'

'I want to give you lots and lots of presents because I haven't been able to do that for a long time.'

'Can Mummy come? Can we go and show Mummy, now?' asked Gemma.

'Of course we can,' said Harold.

He stopped and turned and they began to retrace their steps. As they walked, he wondered briefly what it would be like to speak with her again after so many years. Not that it mattered that much... Carri had been restored to him. Carri loved him and was leading him by the hand out of the darkness, away from the wilderness.

They reached the far side of the precinct and he spotted Gillian. Evidently, she had finished her conversation and had moved over towards the tree. There was no sign of her friend, but she was at the centre a small crowd and seemed to be gesticulating and throwing her arms in the air. Same old Gillian then, always theatrical about something or other... Or was it possible that *finally*, after all of these years, she had come to recognise just what she had done?

He smiled down at Carri and she hugged the doll tightly and smiled right back at him. He would never let her go; however, it was the Season of Goodwill... They would go over to Gillian and he would comfort her and try to find some small space in his heart to forgive.

3

Christmas Comes to Knarebridge

Christmas was coming and people in Knarebridge-on-the-Moor could talk of little else. Three days of heavy snow had caused severe disruption across the region and the village was all but cut off from the outside world. The cold snap could not possibly have come at a worst time. The ploughs were contesting the white-out conditions on the bleak surrounding hills, but whenever a promising swathe of road was reopened, an obstinate wind piled back the drifts.

Many of the villagers were panic-buying, others were simply battening down for the duration. Some had made plans to escape to relatives, or sunnier climes, but the weather had shown no sign of releasing its grip and now Christmas was bearing down upon them and all faced the prospect of remaining trapped for the duration.

Within the inner precinct of the village, the snow had at least been cleared. The narrow streets were choked with shoppers. Chaos and pandemonium reigned as, neighbour contested neighbour, for the dwindling provisions that remained. Sergeant Anthony Reynolds was alone in his task of attempting to restore sanity to the High Street. Despite the terrifying events of four years past, the Yorkshire Constabulary had not seen fit to increase police presence in what was, after all, a village of only five hundred souls. His advice to all in the current circumstances was simply to keep calm, go home and lock the door on a hostile world.

'You'd think they were stocking up for World War Three,' said John Ackroyd to his wife, as the queues formed and reformed through the doorway of their village mini-market. He handed her a steaming mug of tea. It had been a day to remember. It seemed to John, that Christmas and the vile weather had brought out the very worst in people.

'I'll take over now,' he told her, whilst glancing out at the brightly-lit High Street. 'Perhaps you could do a little shelf-filling; that's if there's anything left to bring out?'

As the mini-market was of a modern, advanced design and practically ran itself, despite their advancing years, the Ackroyds had always managed alone. Such had been the current demand however, that at lunchtime, Mary had had need to call in Jenny, her young niece to help out. As darkness fell, Jenny's father had turned up to collect her. It was understandable. At such a time he wanted her home, safe in the bosom of the family.

'I'm closing on the dot at seven thirty,' said, John resolutely, 'and wild horses wouldn't drag me into opening tomorrow.'

It was such a statement of the obvious, but his wife nodded her vigorous agreement. No one else would be opening next day either, and it was not as if there would be much left to sell.

'At least it will be a chance for a decent rest,' she said comfortingly. 'We'll slide the bolts, put up the bars and sit like two bugs in a rug in front of the telly.'

Mary liked to mention the bolts and bars, it gave them both some much needed reassurance. Four years had passed, but despite the extensive counselling, neither she nor, John, had ever fully recovered from the terrifying break-in. She had only to close her eyes to see the mad, staring face of the knife-man before her. Had it not been for Sergeant Reynolds happening by for his pipe tobacco, and hearing noises from the back of the shop... Mary shuddered and tried to put such thoughts from her mind.

Knarebridge was about as ready as it could be for Christmas. It stood out like an oasis of light against the bleak wilderness of the moors. In normal times, only the illuminated church spire would have pinpointed the village, but now even the humblest cottage was a beacon of light and colour.

Sergeant Reynolds timed his call for closing time; he had made it a habit ever since the assault. He parked up as close to the mini-market entrance as possible and the chains on his wheels dug deeply into the snow-pile. It was not a night to be walking far. There were double-yellow lines beneath the snow, but there are special rules for policemen and these were extraordinary days.

'Evening both. How's it going?' he asked.

'Just about ready to lock up, Tony,' answered, John Ackroyd. 'We've been rushed off our feet.'

'At least it's good for business, then?'

John nodded soberly. 'So, what's new – anything?'

The officer shrugged. 'Nothing to speak of.'

'Christmas again and we're all blocked in... I just can't believe it,' said Mary, with feeling.

'Yep. There we are,' agreed the sergeant. 'The sooner we get back to normal, the better.'

The very thought of Christmas, upset him: the extra vigilance, the additional shifts, the pitiful lack of help and back-up. He struggled to raise a smile, to appear cheerful, but his mind was elsewhere. He picked up his pipe tobacco and made to leave.

'At least have a cup of tea with a little something to strengthen it?' offered Mary.

'Best not, thanks all the same. I've a long night ahead, wouldn't do to be woolly-headed.' He turned and headed for the door.

'You take extra care now, Tony,' said John.

'I will. I will. You too – and that lovely wife of yours. Get yourselves battened down now, nice and cosy and forget it all.'

The street outside was as bright as day, but deserted now. No one saw the man in the white fatigues sneak from behind the mini-market and climb into the back of the police car. He closed the door quietly behind himself and crouched down into the foot-well. Seconds later, Sergeant Reynolds exited the shop, stepped over the small snow-bank and slid in behind the wheel. He placed his tobacco on the front shelf, keyed the ignition and drove off slowly down the High Street.

The police station car park was in semi-darkness, shielded from the street by a high wall. Half an hour remained before he was due to contact the external search teams. Time for a quiet pipe. Best stay in the car, the station had been empty all day and would take ages to warm up... Hours of vigilance lay ahead.

'Bloody Christmas!' he cursed, as he stuffed the bowl of his pipe. There was the day's log to complete. He switched on the interior light, picked up the book and began to thumb the pages. *More problems:* 'No February the twenty-ninth...'

He growled aloud. The log didn't accommodate the additional Leap Year day... He would *have* to go inside now and search out a blank page to complete the day's entry. He cursed again roundly and reached for the door handle.

The figure on the back seat arose silently and plunged the knife deep into the neck of Anthony Reynolds. The spinal cord severed between the third and forth vertebrae and the policeman died before his final breath had escaped him.

John Reginald Halliday Christmas had made good the threats that he had screamed out in court. *February the twenty-ninth* – four years to the day. Against the odds, he had broken out of his padded cell in Broadmoor and evaded all pursuit. The weather had aided the ex-SAS man; he had blended into the snows like a ninja and returned to his home village, to avenge himself upon the bobby who had put him away.

Mistletoe – as he was known inside – cleaned his knife carefully on the dead man's clothing. The excitement had made him hungry. It was time to make a return to the mini-market...

Things were looking up. He was beginning to feel like a very happy Christmas.

4

Claus Noel

Bensons was the largest store on the High Street and the target of Claus Noel's research. He returned the advert to a copious pocket in his red, fur-lined coat and strode in through the impressive, automatically operated, double entrance doors.

'Get him!' said Chrissie of Cosmetics to Patty of Perfumery. For the first time that morning, she had stopped doing her nails – but only for as long as it took to gape at the rotund, bearded figure who was passing by her counter.

'A bit early, innee?' parried Patty, in a monumental monotone of undisguised disinterest.

Mr Benson's secretary found the man's appearance and strange accent most disconcerting and was all but poached by the waves of her hot flushes. So anxious was she to deflect the piercing stare of his lavender-field eyes that she reversed into her own waste bin, fell heavily against Mr Benson's office door and hurtled unannounced, onto his deep pile carpet.

George Benson glanced over the edge of the *Financial Times* and deftly secreted his copy of *Girls Go Wild* between its folds.

'Intercom too low-key for you today then, Charlotte?' he mused.

'Oh no... I mean, yes – that is... Can I have a personal word, Mr Benson?'

'You may rise and approach,' he encouraged, although it was plain to him that in the circumstances, his celebrated sense of humour was squandered upon the poor creature.

'Sir, it's just that we have a Father Christmas in Reception, enquiring about the job.'

'Yes, and-?'

'Well, Sir – he's turned up in full uniform.'

'Has he, *by George!*' exclaimed George. It was an expression to which he felt greatly attached.

'What shall I do, Sir?'

'Well, I think perhaps you'd better wheel him in.'

The flustered Charlotte blushed and brushed herself down in equal proportions, before retreating backwards through the door, to appear again almost instantaneously, with the imposing stranger.

George Benson sifted through his armoury of welcoming smiles and chose a well-crafted, professional, semi-toothed little number, signifying a low-key mix of patronising superiority and affected warmth and friendship.

'Good morning to you,' he said, whilst proffering a well-manicured hand across the desk. 'George Benson, owner and chief executive of Bensons, and you are?'

'Noel. Claus Noel. I am coming from the North Pole and enquiring of the newspaper proposal and pleased to be making your acquaintances.'

"Very droll, Mr Noel, very droll! And what an appropriate handle for the job. A nom-de-plume, I take it? Ha, ha!'

Claus looked slightly puzzled. 'I am not speaking much of the French... will it be a requirement?'

'Sticking with the humour, are we? Always useful... I *do* like the uniform. We provide one, of course, but I see that yours is rather more splendid.'

'That is relieving, I would not be wishing to wear someone else's clotheses,' said Claus, blissfully unaware of his grammatical idiosyncrasies.

'Settled then, as you've taken so much trouble over today.'

'I am coming for the job?'

'Yes, yes... I think we've gone beyond that; though I must point out that the start date is not before the fifteenth.'

'That would be acceptably acceptable,' said Claus. 'I have much working back at the North Pole, before.'

George Benson was grinning from ear to ear. 'I'm relieved that you're not one of those dour, Bergmann types – the ones who act like Odin with earache.'

'I know Odin well; he can also be genially highly genial.'

'You're a dry one, Claus, to be sure! I hope the kids will catch on with it all.'

'I am having the task then?'

'You are most certainly having the task, as you say – subject of course, to references... Maybe Odin can come up with one? Ha, ha, ha.'

'He is hardly the appropriate personage,' replied Claus. 'I have been researching also in the stores of Austria and Germany... they will bring an affirmation of my worthiness.'

'Wonderful thing, this European Union,' said George.

'To the fifteenth,' replied Claus, and with a swirl of his magnificent fur-lined, red cloak, he brushed heavily against the wilting Charlotte, before making his dramatic exit.

George Benson dined out on the story for a couple of weeks, but he harboured no expectations of ever seeing the intriguing Mr Noel again... To his surprise, impeccable references soon arrived from Vienna and Berlin; if continental opinion was to be believed, Claus Noel was indeed a rather wonderful Father Christmas.

It was George Benson's habit to arrive well before his store's opening time. On Saturday December the fifteenth, he found Claus Noel in full uniform, sitting on the marble entrance steps. Making full use of the opportunity, George walked him around the empty store. Proudly, he showed off the Fantasy Forest, where children would arrive, en-route to Santa's Grotto on the Snowy Mountain. Harrods could have done it no better, he confided and his new Father Christmas seemed inclined to agree.

Once alone, Claus busied himself checking out the quality of the gifts and arranging the snowy kingdom to his own satisfaction. Shortly after opening time, a grossly overweight young man with acne came by, to make his acquaintance.

'I'm, Brian, from Bedding,' the man announced. 'I'm your lunchtime relief. If the pips begin to squeak in between times, just give me a shout.'

'I shall not be squeaking any pips,' Claus replied.

Brian had been warned that Claus Noel was somewhat eccentric, so he tried again. 'Have you met Rosie? She'll be taking the gate money at Fantasy Forest; she'll let me know if you need any extra help.'

'I shall not be needing of the help and the relief,' announced Claus, ungraciously.

Brian was slow to take offence, but this seemed plain rude. 'Suit yesself, mister. What with the cold snap, there's plenty to do in Bedding. Mr Benson says I should cover lunchtime − for the rest of it, you can paddle your own canoe.'

'I am not knowing of any water transportation,' replied Claus, further perplexed.

'Very funny! Have you ever thought of going on the stage?'

Even by coffee time, Brian had not fully regained his composure. He took himself off to the canteen for a comforting: *Bensons' Home-baked, jam and cream-filled, organic doughnut - contains no additives or artificial flavours. Sourced from local suppliers* and sat chewing morosely.

Rosie arrived with uplifting news: a coach-load of infants from an inner-city improvement project had arrived without prior notification – a total of forty children in all – and Claus was making heavy work of them. Brian nodded with justifiable satisfaction... but could see no good reason to be rushing to the foreigner's assistance.

At the appointed hour, Brian arrived at the entrance to the Grotto, to provide the prescribed lunch-time cover. The last few of the tearaways from the coach party were screaming and shouting their way towards the exit and he was gratified to see *despair* written upon, Claus's face. His red coat was soiled and his hair was streaked and pitted with ice cream and candy-floss. Clumps of his beard had been harvested by probing little hands. He had been pinched, poked, pulled, prodded, patted, punched, piddled-on and provoked. Even now, a random four year old was biting viciously upon his forearm whilst her brother sicked-up on his tunic. He was bruised, battered, sticky, sicky and mightily in need of the respite.

Hattie, from the canteen was hugely empathetic. She served him a: *Bensons' Exclusively selected from carefully approved third-world organic growers, lap sang soo chong – a coarse-leafed tea.* in a cracked cup with a lip-stick streaked rim.

'Prental control's gone, Claus,' she said sorrowfully. 'And the bloomin' teachers 'ave their 'ands

35

tied. No smackin' no more, see... Don't know what the world's a-coming to, I really don't.'

Claus stroked the remains of his beard and struggled diligently to ascertain precisely what language the kind lady was speaking. Hattie returned his gaze. She was fairly sure that he agreed with the general thrust of her sentiments, but it was always a bit awkward with foreign gentlemen who had yet to master the finer points of the Queen's English.

With a portion of: *Bensons' Shepherds' pie – made-exclusively from certified British pedigree herds with natural flavourings of herbs and spices* lying heavily upon his stomach, Claus made a reluctant return to the Grotto. All was quiet, Brian had no customers. He handed back control to Claus with an air of professional disdain.

Before long, the crowds returned and Claus had his back to the wall again.

'I am coming from Lapland and so I have accent, same as you have different accent, same as everybodys,' he was trying to explain to a xenophobic toddler – but young Lucy appeared wholly unconvinced. She delivered an experimental kick to his shin. It was a professional foul worthy of the Premier League, precision-aimed for maximum pain. In the immediate thrall of agony, Claus dropped his young charge on the floor of the Grotto. Lucy's wail carried the decibels of three police sirens, more than enough to register upon the maternal antenna at the far side of Fantasy Forest. Mum entered the Grotto with murder in mind and Claus was saved only by the quick thinking

Rosie: the good lady was persuaded to accept with bad grace, an additional four presents and a full return on her daughter's entrance fee.

Claus had hardly time to reassemble a modicum of calm and a measure of equilibrium before tiny Steven Andrews took justifiable exception to the proffered plastic pistol.

'Got one already,' he informed Claus, prior to blinding him temporarily with a prodigious jet-stream of spittle.

Claus was tired and hurting. 'Too bad,' he hissed. 'All that is lefted. Sorry.'

It was perhaps predictable that Steven felt the need to give vent to his burgeoning sense of injustice. He rammed the silver barrel of the offending gift into Claus's left nostril, with sufficient force to ensure that its trajectory was arrested only by the ultra-sensitive gristle of the septum. Had Claus been in any condition to make an objective comparison, he would have recognised perhaps, a certain compensatory therapeutic effect upon his damaged shin and masticated wrist.

As Rosie bathed his injury, she tried her best to look on the bright side.

'Never mind,' she said. 'At least, the blood blends in with your lovely red uniform. You don't notice the cotton wads in your nose either, they're the same colour as the remains of your beard... You are talking a bit funny though...'

It was of little comfort; his attention was fixed upon the arrival at the Grotto entrance, of the *North Oxminster Infants' Heavenly Gospel Choir.* Eighteen in number and having just completed a vocal stint in *Women's Clothing,* they were all intent upon seeing Father Christmas...

Only Chrissie and Patty saw him leave. They commented that he had looked quite out of sorts, as he swept through Cosmetics and Perfumery. He failed to show up on the following Monday, claimed no wages and was never seen or heard of again, in Oxbridge.

A few days later, the children of Britain opened their eyes to Christmas morning; but oh! − how rapidly their joy and wonder turned to dismay and despair. In every house, in every street, in every town throughout the land, there wasn't a single Christmas present to be found − not a name tag, nor ribbon, nor shred of wrapping paper.

Meanwhile across the rest of the world, a different story was unfolding. Children were shouting their joy to the rooftops, as puzzled parents struggled to decipher English messages on the many additional presents, that had simply appeared out of nowhere.

5

The Best Christmas Ever

The intimate seasonal domestic cocoon closed in
tightly and there was no hiding place for Ted and
Imelda Muzurki. Recent wounds broke open, new
warts and whorls appeared and old scars itched
intolerably. They prepared their individual Christmas
dinners in malevolent silence. Imelda feasted upon
turkey breast in white wine sauce with all of the
trimmings and followed it with mini-Christmas
pudding and brandy butter. Ted made beans on toast
garnished with a sprig of holly and washed it down
with the warm lager that Imelda had excluded from the
fridge.

Ted was a concept artist, Imelda, an actuary.
Ted was a hopeless romantic, Imelda, intensely
grounded and practical. Her dour, matter-of-fact, no
frills approach to life depressed Ted and repressed his
sunny, optimistic nature. Ted's slap-dash, devil-may-
care attitude towards even the most pressing of
everyday issues, drove Imelda to distraction and
despair. They had spent the Festive Season ratcheting
down the coffin lid on their failing, ill-matched
marriage and both knew that this would be the last of
their "shared" Christmases.

Following three days of barbed words and long silences, they entered the dog days between Christmas and the New Year, when the gloomy dawn seems hardly distinguishable from the returning dusk. Ted spent the time in the solitude of his room, chewing on daily culinary disasters with only his laptop for company. It was then that he made himself a solemn vow: Never Again! Next year, come what may, he was going to have *the best Christmas ever.*

January hobbled in with sleet and fog. Cold relief. From her side, the divorce was bitter, acrimonious and vengeful. He took no interest in his counsel's arguments and advice, or in the proceedings themselves. He simply wanted out and by the fastest route possible. Predictably, her lawyers exploited every unguarded opportunity and skinned Ted almost down to his last penny. Imelda was awarded the house and most of their savings, but at least there was no claim for maintenance, her own substantial income was more than enough to fulfil her needs.

Ted left the matrimonial home taking only his car, laptop and a single suitcase. He was free to start over. After three days in a cheap hotel, he found a room to rent with a shared bathroom, above a barber shop. Bleak days followed, black and white hours spent working on the few commercial commissions that remained in his portfolio. He hung on in only by remembering his Christmas vow; it gave some vague point to life and the faint hope that he had turned a corner.

More commissions followed and finally, the offer of a permanent job; the chance to escape the insecurity of freelancing and an all important boost to his finances and morale. *Delta Force* made computer games and Ted's job would be within a team that conceptualised and designed the robots, monsters and heroes that the animators brought to life. Within a month, he was able to say goodbye to his humble lodgings and move to a town-centre flat.

With new money in his pocket, Ted took to lunching at a diner close to his workplace. No one else from the firm used it; it was a little too up-market for the pay grade, but Ted figured he deserved it. The waitress was a sweet girl called Althea – her name was emblazoned upon her white blouse, and the 'th' in the middle, dipped sweetly and provocatively into the valley of her bosom. Althea was *his* waitress and each day as he watched her rhythmic progression backward and forward to his table, he allowed himself to fantasise far beyond the images that he used in the games industry. Althea seemed to be everything that Emelda had not been: she was cheerful rather than doleful, chatty rather than morose, witty rather than dull and upbeat rather than downbeat. She was also blonde and beautiful with an hourglass figure. Althea was in fact, the woman of his dreams.

Ted went to the diner whether hungry or not, and as spring turned to summer he began to put on a little weight. To his way of thinking, it was a price well worth paying. He observed her intently and worried when dark rings appeared under her eyes and some of

her earlier sparkle appeared to go missing. *Was* it his imagination, or was she looking more careworn? –
Then came the day when Althea was absent altogether from his table and he was served by the manager himself. It underlined to him, the true depth of his feelings. Before the end of the meal, he just had to ask:

'What's happened to Althea?

'She's been going through a difficult divorce, Mr Muzurki,' replied the man soberly. 'She's taking two weeks annual leave, to recover.'

'Oh, my goodness... I'm so sorry to hear that,' replied Ted, solicitously. He shook his head slowly and sadly. He had never pictured himself as an actor, but now he realised that he was gilt-edged Oscar material. *How had he managed to keep a straight face, when his legs had wanted to dance a jig and he'd felt like planting a kiss on the man's forehead and buying everyone a round of drinks?*

Althea returned in due course and he risked telling her how much she had been missed. With feigned innocence and a guilty smile, he enquired whether she had enjoyed her holiday... To his secret delight, she confessed that the absence had been due to personal reasons. She did not elaborate and of course, he did not press. He was on the case now. At some point during the following week, he managed to slip into their daily discourse the fact that he was divorced. Althea rewarded him with the most priceless phrase that he could ever remember: "Me too".

He fought to reign himself in. Easy... easy. What was she – twenty-five? There was a good twenty years between them. Maybe she was merely being friendly and polite to a regular customer? But oh! How things had changed for him: for the first time in years, he felt truly alive. He could begin to think and plan and dream again. *Dream again*... His Christmas promise came flooding back and now he knew for certain: there was only one person with whom he could share it. He began to hope and save and plan in earnest.

Autumn came and went, the days grew shorter and Christmas drew near. The tangible, calculable reality proclaimed by hoardings and shop windows, winked and blinked from street decorations and carolled by choirs. For Ted Muzurki, it was going to be the Christmas of all Christmases! Now, all had been planned. Althea would be joining him for lunch and afterwards, who *knew* where that could lead?

He awoke on the day to joyous anticipation. Everything had to be perfect. He took a tour of the brightly decorated flat and his chest filled with pride. The log fire in the ornate brass grate glowed brightly, casting its heat across the polished pine floor. Artfully concealed lighting provided just the right romantic atmosphere. Soft furnishings, drapes, rugs and ornate cushions added to the slight air of oriental mystique. The turkey was slow-cooking already and its rich aroma mingled with the joss that smouldered from hidden nooks and crannies.

She would be arriving soon... He checked and rechecked the Christmas table: serviettes, silverware, bone china, crystal glasses, seasonal tablecloth, two place settings – hers with a view of the gardens – fine wine already uncorked; although of course, they would begin with the mulled wine. All underway for *the best Christmas ever.*

She was here! In the driveway – his fantasy woman had arrived. His spirits soared as she paid off the taxi and headed for the front door. Quickly, he moved out of sight. The flat was ground floor, it wouldn't do to appear too keen. The bell rang and he forced himself to count to twenty before opening. Satisfied, he checked the flower in his button hole and pulled down the handle.

Althea looked a living dream: every man's idea of the perfect woman. Her bright yellow off-the-shoulder dress perfectly highlighted her corn-blonde hair, a black lace shawl thrown loosely about her shoulders added a Madonna-like quality to her faultless features. He had thought her unattainable, but had refused to surrender his dream and here she was – with him on Christmas Day!

As she smiled her greeting, she glanced upwards at the hanging mistletoe. 'Mustn't let it go to waste,' she told him and kissed him lightly on the cheek. Ted's cup ran over.

She paused again at the lounge door and gazed around with sparkling eyes. 'Wow! Really impressive. You must have worked so hard... It's beautiful... and what taste. Mmm... the smell of that cooking! It certainly beats the diner. I had no idea that you were so accomplished.'

It was exactly the reaction for which he had been hoping. 'Come over to the tree, I have something for you,' he said.

He bent beneath the branches and passed over the carefully wrapped parcel. Her eyes shone with the excitement of a little girl.

'I have something for you, too,' she responded, reaching into her handbag. Ted caught sight of the kisses on the gift label and once again, his heart bounced and his head swam.

He led her to the deep settee beside the glowing fire and they endeavoured to unwrap their gifts simultaneously. Two watches – almost identical, *his and hers*. It brought a merry peal of laughter from Althea's beautiful lips. To his astonishment, she leant forward and gave him his second kiss of the morning.

'Thank you,' she said, 'and thank you for the invitation... I couldn't be happier.'

Ted struggled to wrench himself from the settee for long enough to fetch the mulled wine. Soon they were back to their new-found intimacy, supping upon the spicy warmth and gazing at the spitting logs. The pain of the past few months was lifting from him like mist on a summer's morning. It was too good to be true, Althea here beside him.

'We should eat,' he told her, with a nod in the direction of the waiting banquet.

'Sit tight,' she replied. 'The very least I can do is to serve the food.'

Ted contented himself with opening the champagne and topping the crystal glasses to just below the rims, as Althea busied herself loading the plates with his delicious Christmas repast. Throughout the meal, despite the noisy crackers and party poppers and the silly hats and the excitement of igniting the Christmas pudding, they had eyes only for each other.

'To happy days,' he murmured as they finished the last of the champagne.

She raised her glass to his. 'Make a wish,' she said and they were quiet again, lost in the wonder of each other's company.

Later, they returned to the fireside, where he poured aromatic South American coffee into little clay cups and opened the Armagnac, to accompany it. She sipped delicately and inclined her golden head upon his shoulder. With bated breath, he enclosed her free hand within his own and was rewarded with a welcoming squeeze.

They sat for a while, making small-talk, exchanging intimacies, but Ted was finding it difficult to control the rising desire that had lain subdued, those many weeks. As if reading his mind, Althea turned her beautiful face towards him.

'Ted,' she asked, 'I don't know how else to put this... but, would you make love to me?'

His pulse rocketed, his breathing grew laboured and his throat constricted. He had never known such excitement. Althea's loving expression began to turn to concern.

'If you don't want to? It's been wonderful, but-'

'Are you sure?' he managed.

'Perfectly sure,' she replied with a smile.

They arose and linked arms and he led her across the lounge, into the hall and along the corridor towards his ornate bedroom with the intimate low lighting. He paused at the door and looked to her again, for confirmation.

She smiled her encouragement. 'It will be fine,' she said, as she moved forward. He swallowed hard, gratified by her eagerness and reassurance.

'Shall I undress?'

'Shall I undress?'

'Shall I undress?'

'Bugger!' yelled Ted, as he struggled to rip the virtual reality helmet from his head. 'Of all the bloody times for a *malfunction!*'

He was alone. The tiny flat was empty, freezing, untidy and bare. He had spent every last penny upon the helmet... There was nothing for it, other than to open his last can of baked beans, jump into his sleeping bag and hope to God that the darned thing would start working again by Boxing Day.

6

Christmas Alone

In the immediate aftermath of the accident, Angela
Drummond wished only that she could have joined
Robert... A foggy November morning on the M25 had
taken from her the man of her life, her soul-mate and
partner of twenty-four wonderful years. There had been
no children; it was selfish perhaps, but so complete in
each other's company had they been, that no vacuum
had ever arisen to primp their parental instincts.

A full three months passed before she surfaced
sufficiently to consider a return to work. Her Director-
General had been most understanding throughout and
now, he had a surprise in store:

'Over the telephone, you've mentioned that
ideally, you'd like a fresh start somewhere, Angela?' he
reminded. 'Well, I've a proposal that I'd like you to
think over. You know of our Research Centre in Lagos,
Nigeria? The position of Chief Research Officer has
become vacant there. If you were so inclined, I'd be
happy to recommend you for the job.'

As recommended, Angela took her time over
her decision: there were no close family ties to consider
− her only sister lived in Sydney, Australia; both
parents had passed on and Robert's father was well-
looked after by his remaining, unmarried son. There

were cherished friends of course... but most of them had been mutual to her and Robert and now tended only to trigger painful reminders of her loss. Perhaps Lagos was exactly what was needed?

Once her mind was made up, Angela began to feel reenergised. For the first time in months, she found herself looking *forward,* making plans and beginning to believe that perhaps there *was* a future after all. She had no real conception of what life was going to be like in Africa, nor into what new dimensions of experience the move would propel her... It would be hot all year round of course, which would suit her fine. It might be possible to live close to the Atlantic beaches, if finances allowed? Lagos was no backwoods, it was Africa's largest metropolis – there would be people to meet, friends to be made, plenty to see and do. She would keep her mind open and allow circumstances to determine much of what she would become. It was all immensely exciting... Robert however, would never be forgotten. In a very real sense, he would travel with her and remain a part of her new self. Her mind was wide-open to challenge and change, but her heart belonged to her husband and was locked firmly against the possibility of new emotional involvement.

Her new research team made her very welcome. Initially, there were so many social invitations that she had to pace herself and to refuse politely almost as many as she accepted. She found herself 'the house by the beach', a modest old colonial building with a history. It was a home that fulfilled one of her longest-standing dreams: to wake each day to the smell of the sea. She joined a gym and a Bridge club and purchased a Jeep. She took up ballroom dancing, something that Robert, with his amiable clumsiness would never have entertained.

Before her first year in Lagos was out, she was feeling fully established – at home – almost part of the scenery. It had been a bold, wise move and was beginning to unlock dimensions of herself that she had hardly recognised were there.

Her relationship with Gerald happened gradually. He was part of the research establishment. She saw him every working day and her feelings for him crept upon her slowly, surreptitiously, unmindfully. For some time, it was no more than a question of looking forward to seeing him each morning, to spending a little time with him over coffee, to walking and laughing with him after lunch. He brightened her day, he tickled her sense of humour. *He* more than anyone, let new light into her soul and by the time she started to miss him at weekends, the die was cast.

It was an incongruous relationship, as Angela was the first to admit: she, an English lady, already into middle-age, quiet, unassuming and conservative in both taste and temperament; Gerald, African-born, still youthful and flamboyant, volatile and quixotic. She was sure that colleagues at work must gossip about them. There were those among her newly-found friends who viewed the relationship with undisguised concern.

As for herself, she quite simply did not care. This was a new Angela. He brought her laughter, a bloom to her cheeks, a sparkle to her eye and a spring to her step − features that had been missing from her life for far too long − and those were diamonds that no money could buy.

As her house was out of town, Gerald's over-night stays became more frequent. It seemed illogical for him not to move in. He had always travelled light and was perfectly at ease with the arrangement.

The move brought about subtle changes in their relationship. Quite quickly, he seemed to develop a sense of ownership, of both Angela and her property. He made it fairly obvious that he cared little for her friends and she noted that there was more than a hint of jealousy whenever they came around.

As for those closest to her, their earliest concerns now began to turn towards palpable disapproval... Angela would hear none of it. Gerald had enriched her life in ways that, following her bereavement, she would never have contemplated could return. She was not about to give up on him and besides − she rather enjoyed having to employ the patient and forgiving side of her nature; it engendered a warm glow of self-approval that was infinitely preferable to the earlier hot tears of self-pity.

Gerald was not slow to appraise the tolerant and forgiving aspects of Angela's nature and began to take full advantage of them. He was easily bored and soon the lure of the town and his old ways became irresistibly seductive. He rejoined former cronies and cruised familiar haunts. He had retained his eye for the opposite sex and Angela was obliged to accept that there were evenings when simply, he did not return.

He did little to hide his quick temper and she learned to try to understand his frustrations and to tread carefully when a mood was upon him... On the night of her fiftieth birthday, Angela gave a small party for her closest friends. None of them had ever felt easy around Gerald, but they knew, it was *Angela and Gerald*, or no Angela at all.

All went well until quite late on; Angela was making coffee prior to people saying their goodbyes: According to the two men who had been with him in the room at the time, Gerald had flown into a rage about some imagined slight – up-ended the dining-room table and stormed from the house into the cloying warmth of the night. There had been no altercation, his behaviour had been quite mystifying.

The women gathered around Angela to comfort her and begged her to consider her best interests.

'You've spoken before of his volatility,' said Gwendolyn Holden, a member of her research team. 'There's no way you should put up with it. Do you really feel safe with his moods, being so far out of town?'

'You don't see the best of him,' sighed Angela. 'There are bad times, like tonight – his behaviour was inexcusable – but most of our days are spent in pure bliss, when he couldn't be more sweet and attentive. He simply makes me so very happy.'

Angela and Gerald remained together. Time passed and he mellowed. Social occasions became more relaxed. Friends no longer expressed their concerns to Angela, or gossiped behind her back. Eventually, he even gave up his philandering and contented himself within her company. Their mutual devotion was apparent to all and finally they were just another couple on the Lagos social circuit.

When Angela retired she began to consider her future anew. At first, she and Gerald settled into a quiet daily routine of walking the beaches and spending the evenings together, listening to the sounds of the night and enjoying the beauty of the Bay, from the veranda. She remained unsettled however. It was as if in her mind, her time in Africa had been wholly associated with her job and now, she hankered for something else.

Over lunch in town one day, she confided her innermost feelings to a close friend. 'It's perhaps morbid and stupid and irrational, but when my time comes, I always imagined being laid to rest in a quiet corner of an English churchyard.'

The thought was out and despite her friend's protestations that she had many more years ahead of her, she knew then that soon, she would return to the country of her birth. Would Gerald want to join her? The question plagued her waking hours. He was so quintessentially *African*. Born, bred and raised to the rhythm of its dark heart. The solution seemed to be for her to travel back first and to try to re-establish herself. Gerald would visit and they would simply have to take it from there... She left with the minimum of fuss and Gerald was left to console himself as best he could, among their many friends.

Within three months, she had settled-in to a pleasant two bed-roomed flat in Wimbledon, that overlooked the common. It was time for his first visit, to discover whether or not he was capable of settling down permanently in England and to adjusting to its climate and the urban London life.

Upon his arrival, her fears on his behalf quickly proved to be unfounded. Day by day, she became convinced that their ongoing relationship was infinitely more important to him, than either geography or climate.

Oddly enough, it was she, herself, who found the readjustment the more difficult. Angela had unearthed no remaining relatives or friends in Britain to fall back upon and despite their renewed togetherness, she felt lonely, isolated and ill at ease. At first, she compensated by writing lengthy letters to her many friends and acquaintances back in Lagos. Sadly, over time, when the replies reduced inevitably to a trickle, she began to withdraw further and further into herself.

The return was ill-fated. By the end of their second London summer, Angela fell ill with a wasting disease. Gerald soon found her depression difficult to cope with and ominously, he returned to the moodiness of his younger days. They gave up their long walks together over the common and spent many hours brooding behind closed doors. How Angela wished that she had never departed from the warmth and sunshine.

Neighbours, who had long-since commented upon the odd couple, now began to complain about unpleasant smells and the accumulation of rubbish outside the flat. Social Services were called in, but Angela quickly sent them packing. Despite her illness and growing infirmity, she retained all mental faculties and had lost none of her gritty, independent character.

The end came on Christmas Eve, as Angela sat in her favourite armchair, listening to *Carols from King's College.* Suddenly, she gazed across lovingly to Gerald, smiled and slipped quietly away. He rose from his chair, crossed to embrace her, then returned to sit, head in hands, beside himself with grief.

He kept his vigil until Boxing Day when the police came around to break into the flat. As he was allowing no one anywhere near to the body, a vet was called to administer a tranquillising dart. When Gerald came to, he was unable to tell anyone his name of course, so one of the policemen christened the elderly chimp: *Charlie Christmas.*

After a lifetime of domesticity, Gerald would never have adjusted to zoo life and after some deliberation, the kindly vet offered him a home. Charlie Christmas lived out the remainder of his days contentedly, but he never, ever forgot his Angela.

7

The Real Father Christmas

Friends on both sides of the Pond envied Sadie's trans-Atlantic lifestyle. She and Charles owned a Chelsea Mews, a Texas ranch and an apartment overlooking New York's Central Park. Their London home was the last word in comfort and luxury. Charles had converted the old stabling into twin, two-storey apartments, one for themselves and the other for his ageing parents. When in England, they found it perfectly adequate.

Given the choice, Sadie would have preferred to spend the Festive Season in Houston, with her parents, but Charles' business interests dictated that they were anchored to London. She had never adjusted to the damp and chill and yearned for the December sunshine of her home State. It was the second year running now, that she had resigned herself to Britain's inevitable winter colds and coughs and sneezes.

There was a more serious downside to her life: Charles lived and breathed for his business enterprises. He was genial when business was on the up, but of late, his drinking had increased and he had grown cold and uncommunicative. She had long-since traded her bridal dreams of romantic togetherness for the sumptuous rewards of his commercial acumen, but his recent moodiness had pulled them steadily apart. For some time now, the happy family image they projected seemed to her, to be little more than company PR.

It was Christmas Eve, but there had been no question of him joining the family for last minute shopping. It was the day of the firm's Christmas lunch and later, she knew, seasonal business networking around the pubs and clubs of the City would be his overriding priority. For the best part of the day, she had run the gauntlet of the seething West End stores, completing gift-buying for the English side of the equation. There was time enough to think about the folks back home when the January sales came around.

She entered Harrods with the children, to fulfil her promise of a visit to Santa's Grotto. It was so ironic, as Charles had been playing Santa that afternoon for the kids of his executives... to be fair, he *had* invited the family – but it had been clear that their own two would have sussed him out immediately.

She glanced at her watch, she was cutting things fine, they *had* to be home by six. 'Come on kids – up the escalator! We have to be quick.'

Robin and Rebecca needed no second invitation, this was the highlight of their day. "Floor Four, Door Ten", she had been told. At the Grotto, Sadie approached the nearest shop assistant and enquired about admission.

'I'm sorry, Madame, but it's by advanced ticket purchase only and we sold out some days ago,' came the devastating reply.

'What did she say, Mummy,' chorused her six year-olds.

'The lady said that Santa can't see any more children right now. Remember, he has to get back to the North Pole real soon; he's picking up Rudolph and all of the presents.'

Robin and Rebecca howled all the way to the ground floor exit and listened with only half an ear to the firm promise of a quick ice-cream sundae. Rebecca attempted to hold on tight to the doorway on the way out.

'Please, Mummy, please... *please* can we go see Santa Claus?'

As customers stared with disdain at the mewling American infants, Sadie dragged herself, her offspring and her shopping out into the milling crowd. She cursed England, she cursed Christmas and she cursed Harrods, but she reserved most of her spleen for her Brit husband. – Why in *hell* couldn't he have made it after his company lunch? PR. PR. PR! He'd be spending the afternoon soaking up whisky in the taverns, with a bunch of *pin-stripes*.

She calmed herself with an effort and struck out for the Promised Land: *Gelato Mio* on Holland Park Avenue. 'It's just up ahead,' she told the kids. 'Tell you what – you can choose whatever flavours you want.'

As they were about to cross the street, they were spotted by a friend. 'Sadie! Sadie!' she yelled, over the heads of the shopping stream.

Sadie turned and her face registered surprise. 'I thought you were back in Holland for the vacation?'

Nellie van der Meer, was the wife of a Dutch embassy official and the two had become friends through the Priory Health Club, in Chelsea.

'No such luck... Jan's caught up in preparations for the Dutch trade delegation – first week in January.'

'Ah, big-business widows, the pair of us,' said Sadie, wistfully.

Nellie turned to the children. 'Hi kids! Why so glum? It's Christmastime!'

Sadie explained that they were on their way for ice-cream, following the disappointment over Santa. The two women talked on, pleased with their chance encounter and oblivious to the crowds dividing past them, like torrents around a mid-river rock.

Robin's eyes alighted upon Santa Claus. He could hardly believe it. There he was, sitting in a nearby doorway, surrounded by balloons and party poppers and stuff! Mummy was wrong! He hadn't left for the North Pole just yet. Maybe he was feeling sorry they'd missed him and followed them down the street?

'Mummy! Mummy!' Robin tugged urgently upon his mother's arm, but he just couldn't get her attention because the Dutch lady was asking his sister what she wanted for Christmas.

Sadie was straining to hear her daughter's long wish-list above the roar of the traffic. They had to get a move on, there was hardly time now for the ice cream sundae. She glanced to her left for Robin. *No Robin...*

'Robin! Robin! – Help! Nellie, Robin's gone missing!' Sadie was filled with sickening panic. How *could* she have taken her eyes off him?

'Over there!' said Nellie, pointing.

And there he was, crouched in a doorway holding hands with a filthy pavement seller, in a cheap Santa outfit. Sadie flew through the gaps in the crowd, oblivious to the pedestrians she barged aside. She swept up her son with a cry of relief and half-carried, half-dragged him back to Nellie and Rebecca.

'You bad, bad boy!' she yelled, shaking him hard, more out of relief than anger. 'Don't you ever do anything like that again!' She hugged the traumatised child to her chest.

Nellie put a protective arm around the two of them. 'Come on, let's all go get those ice-creams.'

Sadie wiped the last of the tears from Robin's reddened cheeks and kept him no longer from his ice cream. 'You promise you'll never do anything like that again?' she demanded.

'I just wanted to say hello to Santa,' he replied, in a small, tremulous voice.

'But you understand, he *wasn't* Santa? He could have run away with you and I'd have lost you.'

Nellie could see the return of tears. 'Yeah, he was a false one, kids,' she explained. 'You must never talk to a Father Christmas you don't know, because he may be somebody just pretending.'

'But the one at the shop was real,' insisted Rebecca.

'He was,' said Sadie. 'I did tell you. He was in such a hurry to get back to the North Pole. Tonight he has to climb down all of those chimneys.'

'Don't fret. If you dry your tears and promise to be good, he'll be coming to see you, too,' added Nellie.

The children smiled. They liked Nellie, she was nice and kind.

Sadie gulped down her pressed fruit juice. 'Come on kids, eat up!' she said. 'Thanks for everything, Nellie. We really must fly; I've a bunch of company wives coming around for canapés and champagne at seven.'

Back at the mews, the pressure was on. The guests were about to arrive and there was no sign of Charles. It was just too much! They were *his* company wives she was hosting, for God's sake... He was supposed to be home to greet them, before bowing out to look after the children. Her only option was to beg help from her mother-in-law's live-in maid. She crossed her fingers that the girl was still around. Charles' parents had left already for a vacation in Scotland.

'I can give it until nine,' Mette, told her, 'then my boyfriend will be here to pick me up'.

'That's all it will take,' said Sadie, gratefully.

The hassle of additional arrangements was serving only to fuel her growing irritation with her husband's no-show. There was hardly time to speed-change, whilst Mette grabbed the canapés from the fridge and set out everything. The children would have to watch TV upstairs until Mette had time to feed them...

In the event, all went well. The wives clearly enjoyed themselves and became giggly and tiddly. They did express disappointment, of course, in not meeting the *man himself.* Sadie managed to usher the last of them out, just as Mette's deadline approached. With a sigh of relief, she flew up the stairs to find the girl coming to the end of Andersen's, *The Little Mermaid.*

The children were sleepy-eyed, sitting up in bed with their imaginations split between a mermaid and the momentous coming of Santa Claus. The two women kissed them goodnight and on the way downstairs, Sadie handed Mette a fifty-pound note by way of thanks.

Woozy from the champagne and the strain of the day, she closed the door upon the girl and sat down with a large brandy to await the return of her errant husband... Where in hell was he? She was lonely and miserable. In Texas the family would be sitting down to lunch about now... home-reared turkey and all of the trimmings. Her brothers would be playing the fool with their little ones. A hot tear ran down her face. *Where in tarnation was he?* Well, he could shove his English Christmas up his English ass! Oxford carols, Queen's Speech, Boxing Day Hunt – all things British were just fuelling her anger.

Robin and Rebecca sat bolt upright in bed. Was that Santa? Had he come? It sounded like *shouting* from downstairs. The light on the landing shone brightly under their bedroom door. On the Donald Duck alarm clock it said half past twelve.

'I'm scared,' said Rebecca.

'Shall we creep onto the landing and have a look?' whispered Robin.

Together they tiptoed to the door and slowly pulled it open. The shouting was coming from Mummy, at the bottom of the stairs. Curiosity won the day and they wriggled across to the stair-head on their stomachs.

It *was* Santa... but he seemed angry too? He was just standing there with his arms folded across his chest. Mummy was further down the hall. She came towards him now and began shouting again.

'Get out! Go on – I told you, get out!'

She began to hit him on his big red coat, with both hands. Suddenly, Santa pushed her hard and she fell down before him, crying and shouting. Now he was bending down and his white beard was almost touching her face. His face was hidden by the red hood and he was talking very quietly and Mummy was looking scared. When he stood up again he turned and began to kick the front door, very hard.

The children wanted to scream out in terror, but they were almost too frightened to breathe. Slowly, they backed away towards their door. How *could* it be Santa? Santa would never push people over?

'It must be a false one, like this afternoon,' whispered Rebecca.

'I know what to do,' said Robin, protectively. 'You wait here, 'til I come back.'

Robin crept into his parents' room and prayed very hard that he would find what he was looking for. There it was, at the bottom of Mummy's wardrobe. He crept back across the landing to rejoin his sister. The false Santa Claus was pacing up and down now and Mummy was on the floor, hugging her knees and weeping.

Robin slid down the stairs on his tummy and waited until Santa returned up the hall. He gripped very tightly with two hands, just as Mummy had taught him, in Texas. The shot from the little silver pistol passed right through the back of the hood of the false Father Christmas and he began to topple over.

Everybody in Texas should know how to shoot a gun, Mummy had always said... Well, he had shot the false Santa Claus and now they would all be safe until Daddy came home.

8

Double or Quit

Rupert and Rufus Root were twins born under the star of Gemini.

'Roots of a single vine,' father Reggie Roberto Root, rightly, regularly remarked.

Only old Mother Ruby Root could tell Rupert and Rufus apart. Other Root relatives ruefully reported repeated relapses in recognition and would resolutely resort to requests for reappraisal. By repute, Ruby ruled the roost, but Aunt Rula Root rallied to the rescue by rapidly requisitioning red rompers: R for Rupert and R for Rufus; unsurprisingly, the rest of the Roots roundly rebuffed the redundant results of this resolution to the riddle.

`Rupert's the one repeatedly and revoltingly regurgitating his Ribena,' retorted Ruby, reassuringly. Resultantly and regrettably, Rufus randomly resolved to regularly regurgitate Ribena too.

Schooldays provided parallel problems. Rupert soon rued and resented the risible ridicule raised by his name. Rufus too, reported regular ribaldry but *Ruperts* routinely rank with Gilberts, Peregrines and StJohns – long-suffering legatees of preposterously posh prenames, pedantically picked by pushy parents with progeny, progression paranoia.

The twins mastered Maths, engaged in English, hid from History, shone in Science, fizzed at Physics, jogged through Geography, gurgled in German and sparkled in Spanish. Rufus loved soccer and hated rugby, Rupert hated rugby and loved soccer. They were talented wingers - Rupert was right-footed and took to the right wing; Rufus was left-footed and took to the left wing. Father, Reggie Roberto ruminated reverently on the resourceful Root-genes that had countenanced one winger per wing.

In manhood, the Roots followed remarkably related routes. They entered university united, chose the Law, and though double firsts were expected, they gained two, two-twos. Rufus joined *Herbert Fitzpatrick Solicitors,* Rupert was recruited by *Solicitors, Patrick Fitz Herbert.* Tennis doubles champions at twenty two, joint chairs of town twinning too, they were twins through and through.

On the very day that Rufus proposed to Tina Doppel, Rupert entered engagement with Nina Ganger. A joint wedding ensued, with honeymoons in two rooms with a view, in Salou. When Nina had twins, a boy and a girl, Tina had two too, a girl and a boy. Life, through and through was too good to be true.

Then came the fateful Christmas Eve, when Rufus and Rupert debarked for a double or two – hooch and cheroots at the *Twin Feathers,* their joint favourite watering hole. Immediately, it was clear to Rufus that his twin was singularly unaffected by the Season's sparkle.

`What ails thee, Rupert?' he enquired, 'And no double-talk will I truck.'

`I've nullified Nina,' came the shocking reply. `I left her a box of her beloved Belgian bon-bons.'

`Wicked on the waistline, but far from fatal, faithful friend!' said Rufus, relatively relieved and reassured.

`Laced with poison – an untraceable veterinary drug, that can take out a rhinoceros.'

Now Rufus was verily amazed, for only that night, he too had despatched his Dearest – her brass bath tub being deftly wired to the mains supply. What rare and rancid ill-fortune, he fulminated: suspicions may not have surfaced from one fatality, but twin tragedies took credibility a tad too far...

On the car park, Rupert elaborated. `The thing is Rufus old chap, I've fallen hook, line and sinker for the barmaid at the tennis club – young Imogen Image... All is arranged for our getaway tonight, we fly to Toulouse, with too much to lose!'

The last vestige of blood drained vigorously from Rufus's visage.

`Not Imogen, Rupert?' he pleaded plaintively, whilst pulling a pistol from the pleat of a pocket. 'Please say it's not Imogen Image?'

Sounds of a heated argument were heard, then twin gun shots, then silence. Rufus lay with a pistol in the left hand, Rupert lay with a pistol in the right, together in death as they'd been in life. Tina and Nina were discovered in their respective homes, at Cotwall End and Wallcot End. The Coroner recorded a verdict of double murder/suicide. It seemed clear that in the midst of the Festive preparations, both sets of Roots had tangoed and tangled with tragic titanic domestic upheavals.

Identical flight tickets for two to Toulouse, were found in Rupert's pocket and Rufus's wallet, although the Coroner found it a considerable conundrum that neither dead wife had commenced packing. No Root connection was ever made to the two empty suites at the *Toulouse Savoy*. No enquiries were made as to why Mr and Mrs Ben Johnson and Mr and Mrs John Benson had never checked-in.

As for poor Imogen Image, following her Boxing Day breakdown, she was diagnosed paranoid schizophrenic and never recovered. From that day on, she told anyone and everyone prepared to listen that she saw two of two, of everything of *everything*.

9

The Anniversary Trip

Bill Seymour was not known for his impulsiveness. Since beginning work at Lloyd's Bank at the age of sixteen, he had inched his way up through the ranks, to end his career as manager of one of the smaller branches in the Birmingham suburbs. Since retirement, he and wife, Irene had settled down happily in their smart, detached house, to an active life of walking, gardening, tennis, indoor bowling, pub quizzes and winter cruises. To their regret, owing to Irene's infertility, there had been no children; they had always maintained however, that this singular misfortune had been the foundation stone of their inseparable bond.

All had gone well until Irene's illness. For some weeks she had put the lumpiness to the back of her mind. When finally she made mention of it to Bill, he had insisted upon an immediate visit to the GP. The mastectomy that followed was extensive, as there had metastasis to the lymph glands. To their considerable relief, her post-operative prognosis was positive: with ongoing therapy, there was a good chance that Irene would return to full health.

When Bill took her home from hospital at the end of November, he broke the news that he had cancelled their golden wedding anniversary dream holiday. It had been booked it a year in advance and they were to have flown to Sydney during Christmas week, to join the *Pearl of the Sea*, for the second half of its round-the-world cruise.

'I could have made it,' said Irene, bravely.

Bill shook his head decisively. 'You have the chemo' ahead of you, Darling. There was no way... We'll have a nice, cosy Christmas at home; do something special for the twenty-seventh and save the cruise until you're back to full fitness.'

As they faced the numerous out-patient appointments together, throughout the bleak and dreary days of December, Bill felt reassured that he had made the right decision. Irene's progress seemed painfully slow, but she bore the pain and discomfort with fortitude. The one bright spot in her day was the daily visit by Gillian, the wonderful MacMillan nurse, who came to change her dressings. For his wife's sake, Bill did what he could to appear cheerful and optimistic; for much of the time, it was far from how he felt.

During Christmas week, he endeavoured to make the coming festival bright and joyful. He purchased new Christmas lights for the front garden, installed a beautiful Christmas tree in the conservatory, decorated the lounge and stocked the freezer with a luxurious variety of their favourite foods. During one trip to the city centre, he bought Irene the most expensive pair of walking boots that he could find. It would be a few weeks before she could make proper use of them, but he hoped that it would bring reassurance and new confidence.

On the morning of Christmas Eve, Irene awoke feeling tired. 'If it OK with you, Love,' she told him, 'I'll have a lie in. I'm not feeling too brilliant; not at all Christmassy.'

Bill swallowed his disappointment and made his way down to the kitchen for a lonely breakfast. As he sat and idled over his coffee, he wondered how he could find more ways to lift her spirits... They should have been on the *Pearl of the Sea* by now. Maybe he had got it wrong − maybe the cruise would have provided a boost that would have outweighed all medical concerns? Too damned late − Christmas was upon them and their ship had sailed.

He crept back to the bedroom and stood gazing down at her poor tired face. She was so pale, so still... What could he do to make things right? What could he do? What could he do? As he descended the stairs again, it came to him in a blinding flash: what of their honeymoon hotel – *The Red Dragon*, overlooking the beautiful Mawddach Estuary and Barmouth Bay? It would have changed over fifty years but he knew that it was still in business, perched on the mountainside, close to Barmouth Bridge. She had *always* said that she would love to revisit... Barmouth was not even three hours away by car. She would be revitalised, restored, taken back to their romantic beginning. He'd pack her secret present, new walking boots! Why on earth hadn't he thought of it before?

Even as he tapped out the number he realised that it was a fool's errand: Christmas bookings would have been completed *months* before; there was no chance. Too late – a female voice was answering. Apologetically, he began to mumble his enquiry into the mouthpiece.

The hotel receptionist's response was as welcome as it was unexpected. 'You phoned at the right time, Mr Seymour,' she said. 'I've just this second taken a cancellation due to appendicitis. If you're interested, I can offer you the twin room for seven days, through to New Year's Day?'

It was almost too good to be true. A trip that *had* to be made. Bill booked on the spot and went back to Irene directly, to tell her the good news.

As soon as he had packed the car, they were off. The weather was remarkably good and set fair for several days of high pressure, with crisp sunny days and chilly nights.

'Just look at that!' he exclaimed, as they crested the summit of the Dinas Pass and looked left to the sun-kissed peaks. 'Cader Idris... *The King's Seat* it means, in English.'

'I know, Bill, I know,' replied Irene, with a smile. 'You tell me every time we pass this spot.'

'What a mountain! We climbed it on our honeymoon – third day, d'you remember?'

'And I never knew how you found the extra energy!'

'Naughty, naughty!' said Bill, laughing ruefully. 'Oh, I do love you, Irene. I *was* quite the man then, wasn't I?'

'And for me, you always will be,' she replied.

They motored on in thoughtful silence. Down, down, to the Dolgellau by-pass and then left, to pick up the road along the estuary. At last, Barmouth Bridge was in sight and they knew that they were approaching journey's end.

'I wonder if Miss Lloyd-Humphrey is still the manageress?' said Bill.

Irene laughed. 'Bill! – You're talking fifty years back! The poor dear would be in her hundreds by now, if she was still breathing.'

'Tsch... yeah. Silly me! Wishful thinking, I suppose. She was the one who taught me my little bits of Welsh. How good would it be, if we could just turn back the clock and everything was the same again?'

They bantered on happily until Bill spotted the slope that led up to the hotel car park.

'Best make sure the handbrake's fully on,' he said. 'I remember the gradients around here!' He ran around to help Irene out and then grabbed hold of the two suitcases. 'Come on, Love. Let the second honeymoon begin!'

The girl behind the desk was nice enough, but the tall, morose-looking bloke, whom Bill took to be the manager, just seemed to stand there and peer right through them.

'Didn't much like the look of him,' said Bill, once they had reached their room. 'Cold fish. Difficult to believe it's his job to fawn all over the guests and make them feel welcome for Christmas.'

'Who cares?' replied Irene. 'Come and take a look at this view!'

They stood side by side in the window bay, gazing at the beauty of the setting sun. It was an extraordinary dusk for late December; the calm waters of the bay were lit red and the headland past Fairbourne reflected pink against the darkening sky.

'I'm so pleased we're here,' he told her. He slipped an arm about her. 'It's been such a trial, hasn't it — this bloody cancer?'

She brushed away a tear from his cheek.

'Chin up now. The very worst is over, Darling. Let's enjoy our stay and relive all of those memories.'

'I'm not too fussed about the Christmas jollies, you know,' he said. 'Shall we just enjoy the meal and then turn in for an early night?'

'If the weather's the same tomorrow, we could try the Panorama Walk,' replied Irene. 'I think I could probably manage it.'

Bill felt a shiver of pleasure, as her new walking boots came to mind; it was going to be such a special surprise.

They rested awhile and when it was time for Christmas Eve dinner, Bill changed into a smart yellow sports jacket and Irene put on her favourite blue evening dress. She wore the necklace that had been Bill's silver wedding anniversary gift.

As they descended the stairs, Bill felt as though they were newlyweds all over again. There were around a dozen tables in the hotel restaurant and most were occupied by a mix of family groups and young

74

and elderly couples. A waitress showed them to their allotted table. Bill ordered champagne and they dallied awhile over their choices of starters and mains. The miserable manager was standing beside the kitchen door and Bill saw him give them a surly look.

'He's over there, taking it all in; miserable devil!' said Bill, behind his hand.

'Forget and enjoy, Darling. Come on – you promised.'

Irene made her choices and Bill ordered for the two of them. The waitress was a young girl of about sixteen. She appeared awkward and embarrassed and Bill had to repeat the order a couple of times before it sank in. When she had finally seemed to grasp it, she took off dreamily towards the kitchen.

'She should write stuff down if her concentration's so poor,' said Bill, unkindly.

'Poor kid,' said Irene. 'She's a student, I'm sure; probably hired just for Christmas week. I wonder if I was so self-conscious at that age?'

Bill was not entirely mollified. Everything *had* to be perfect, this was their golden wedding anniversary. 'Personally, I'd have been happier with staff that seem a little more professional,' he said grumpily.

Irene laughed. 'You're still hankering after the return of Miss Lloyd-Humphreys.' she told him.

The starters arrived and Bill realised just how hungry he was. The wait had been worthwhile; by the time he had finished his hot Cromer crab in the shell with melted gruyere, he was ready for a few of Irene's

Cardigan Bay mussels in garlic and white wine. The champagne was an ideal accompaniment and he felt his mood lifting. For the main course, they had settled for Venison pie with a delightful assortment of fresh sautéed vegetables. *The Red Dragon* had certainly come on a long way since their honeymoon, but at that time, Welsh catering had not taken up much of their attention.

The delay between main course and sweet was now becoming interminable. Other tables that ordered later were being served and Bill's patience was wearing thin. Irene was looking so tired, despite her bright, brave front. He was keen to get her back to the room, where they could relax over a cuppa and watch Christmas TV.

An opportunity came when the young girl arrived to serve sweet course to the family at the next table. 'I say,' said Bill loudly, 'we've been finished on this table for some time, my Dear.'

The family looked embarrassed and the waitress blushed deeply. 'Oh, you're finished?' she echoed, gauchely. Bill gestured with his open hands at the table.

'Can we perhaps get the sweet sometime soon? We're not fussed about coffee.'

'I'll be with you in a moment, Sir,' she replied, looking all at sea. 'Sorry about that.'

Bill shook his head resignedly. 'It shouldn't have been necessary, you know,' he said loudly. 'Not at the prices we're paying.'

The family next to them kept their heads close to their plates. The waitress arrived back again quickly, but with only one sweet.

'For *Goodness Sake*, Love!' cried Bill, in exasperation. 'It's *two* Melba Supremes! I'd made that perfectly clear – we both ordered the same sweet!'

The unfortunate girl looked close to tears and hurried off to bring a second Melba. The morose-looking manager was staring intently towards their table and Bill mustered up a scowl. In truth, he was beginning to feel quite wretched. Angry with himself for speaking sharply to the kid, who was clearly doing her best; sad to see Irene looking so pale and wan and disappointed that the dream anniversary alternative was not going entirely to plan.

He picked at the cream around a peach and then pushed it aside. 'Come on Darling, I can't finish this anyway. Let's go upstairs and call it a day.'

Bill awoke suddenly, sat bolt upright and checked his watch; it was almost half-past three in the morning.

'Irene! Did you hear that? I'm sure somebody's-'

And sure enough, the bedroom door inched open, creaking loudly on its hinges. The figure of a middle-aged woman appeared, lit by a strange greenish light. Her hair was tied in a bun, she was wearing a large floral apron and carrying a silver tray in her hands.

'Miss Lloyd-Humphrey!' cried Bill. 'You- you *are* still here?'

The apparition glided forward into the room. 'Hello Bill,' it said. 'It's so nice to see you both after all of these years! Look, I've baked *bara brith* for your breakfast.'

'Fruit loaf!' cried Bill. 'You taught me the Welsh name! Look, look, Irene – it's Miss Lloyd-Humphrey!'

Miss Lloyd-Humphrey smiled. 'It was your favourite, remember?' She began to glide backwards towards the open doorway.

'Please don't go!' cried Bill. 'Miss Lloyd-Humphrey, there's so much to talk about.'

He jumped from his bed and followed the disappearing figure out through the bedroom door.

'Miss Lloyd-Humphrey!' he shouted, as he pursued her along the corridor. 'Miss Lloyd-Humphrey!' He stopped at the head of the stairs and shouted down, one more time, 'Miss Lloyd-Humphrey!'

Doors along the corridor had opened and guests were peering fearfully at the man in pyjamas who was making such a commotion in the dead of night. The tall, imposing form of the miserable manager appeared on the floor below. He sized-up the situation rapidly and took the stairs three at a time.

'Mr Seymour!' he hissed through clenched teeth, 'What in hell is going on?' Without allowing Bill time to reply, he grabbed him by the shoulders and began to march him back in the direction of his room. 'Nothing to worry about,' he said, as they passed by the sea of anxious faces. 'Everything under control!'

At the entrance to the bedroom, Bill managed to grab a doorpost, to prevent himself from being pitched inside.

'Will you *listen*. I really did see her... it was Miss Lloyd-Humphrey, the previous manageress here.'

'Mr Seymour, please! That's quite enough. There was no one out here, I can assure you! And no one's ever heard of a Miss Lloyd-Whatever... Now calm down and get some rest.' He practically pushed Bill back into his room and closed the door firmly upon him.

Bill stood in the middle of the bedroom, feeling confused. He turned to Irene. 'But I *did* see her,' he cried. 'She was standing just here, as plain as day, as real as you and me. Please tell me you saw her, Irene?'

Irene arose from the bed, crossed the room and put an arm around him. 'Come and lie down now, Love. Don't upset yourself. To be honest, it might have been just a dream. You were thinking about her only yesterday evening and you've been under so much strain lately.'

Bill finally slept. When he awoke, it was already nine and his head ached from the champagne. The sun was shining brightly through their window. Irene was up, dressed and sitting reading.

'Ohhh... why didn't you wake me?' he asked.

'You were sleeping like a baby, Darling. It would have been a crime,' said Irene. 'Do you want to shower later? – If you put on something, we can go and enjoy a nice Christmas Morning breakfast.'

'I *did* see her, Irene,' he murmured, as they descended the stairs.

They entered the dining room and it seemed to him that a number of people were giving them none too friendly stares.

'Well, it looks like you must have made your mark last night,' commented Irene with a smile.

'Anyone would think I'd murdered somebody,' said Bill, gloomily.

'And as I've said before,' replied Irene, 'take no blooming notice!'

'Full English, for both of us,' said Bill to the waiter, 'Or I suppose I should say Welsh?' He looked for an acknowledgement, but the man merely appeared to roll his eyes, before walking away.

'Don't even know whether he's taken the order,' thundered Bill. 'What the devil's the matter with 'em, Irene? – It's Christmas morning and *Party Time* according to the notice in the lobby. You'd think that we were at a damned funeral!'

He was speaking quite loudly again and heads were turning. No one was laughing.

'And *yes!*' he announced to all who cared to listen, 'I did see a ghost and not I'm not happy with this place. I'm not usually in the habit of complaining but the darned service here has been appalling!'

The waiter returned, carrying only the first of the breakfasts. Bill exploded with anger.

'For God's Sake, not again? Don't you ever cook *two* meals at a time here?'

He spotted the manager, scowling by the kitchen door and jumped up from the table. The man turned on his heel as Bill approached and walked out towards Reception.

'Hey!' roared Bill. 'I want a word with you!'

The manager was waiting for him in the foyer. 'I'd like a word with you too, Mr Seymour. But, well away from the other guests.'

'You're ruining our wedding anniversary!' shouted Bill. 'I've never experienced anything like it... We came here expecting the very best of Christmases.'

'And *you*, Mr Seymour, are damaging my business.'

'If you are referring to last night, I can assure you that Miss Lloyd-Humphrey-'

'Enough! Mr Seymour.'

The manager held up his arms dramatically. 'You can walk with ghosts, talk with ghosts and meet ghosts on every street corner as far as I'm concerned – but not in *my* hotel!'

'She was there, damn you! There in that corridor.'

'You have left me no choice, Sir. I must ask you to pack your bags and vacate the hotel.'

'How dare you threaten me! You have no idea how ill my wife has been!'

'I am truly sorry to hear that, Sir. However, it is no threat that I'm making – it is an instruction... I'm willing to offer a full refund, but I must *insist* upon your departure. I have both the authority and the legal right to eject any guest that I deem to be disruptive and that is precisely what I intend to do.'

Bill stopped the car at the summit of the Dinas Pass and turned lovingly to Irene.

'I meant what I said; I intend to sue, you know.'

She smiled and took his hand.

'It was short and sweet, but you *did* cause quite a fuss, my Love. We have our memories though, Bill, and now you can hold on to them all.'

He smiled sadly. 'Would that it could have been longer.' He kissed her tenderly. 'Let's go home, Irene. I do love you, so.'

As Bill pulled into the driveway of his house, he took note of the police car parked nearby. Before he could place the key in the front door, Gillian, Irene's Macmillan nurse, opened from the other side.

'Bill! Bill – Oh, thank goodness... I've been so worried about you.'

He nodded sadly, but made no reply.

'So, where have you been these past two days?'

'Barmouth,' said Bill. 'For our second honeymoon.'

A policeman appeared around the lounge door and extended his hand. 'Good afternoon, Sir. I'm PC Woodman. Gillian, here, called us when she- when you were- I'm so very sorry for your loss, Sir.'

'I found Irene, upstairs,' said Gillian, in a whisper. 'It must have been such a terrible shock to you.'

Bill looked back wistfully at the empty passenger seat of his car.

'It would have been our golden wedding anniversary on Wednesday,' he told them.

10

George Reed's Christmas Tour

George Reed was a self-made man. 'Fortune smiles on the prepared mind,' he was fond of saying and no one could ever have accused him of not adhering to his maxim... A degree in *Business Studies* at LSE was followed by a Harvard doctorate in *Strategic Macro-Economics,* after which, George had felt ready to take on the world. In the early years, he had specialised in seeding new enterprises. Later, he formed his own group of companies, gathering around himself a think-tank of brilliant young commercial minds, from which he harvested and developed further world-beating ventures. They were frenetic, exciting times and as his fortune grew, he expanded vertically and horizontally into manufacturing, franchising and real estate. It took skill, boundless energy and a certain Darwinian ruthlessness; qualities that his bankrupted rivals met up with, to their cost.

Over time, his growing organisational infrastructure led to the appointment of echelons of technicians and corporate managers; inevitable developments that weaned George reluctantly from the sharp end, where his primary motivation had been sited. Saddled with the growing remoteness of his presidential role and with nothing more to fill his days than the relatively low-level demands of corporate strategy, George turned the focus of his undiminished energy to high spending and high living.

He never married, though there were affairs aplenty. He was a ladies' man, but was always too fly to allow any one woman to stake her claim. His house parties on both sides of the Atlantic became legendary and de rigour for international A-grade celebrities. He was the friend, playmate and confidante of the great, the good, the not-so-good and the downright shady.

The global glitterati awaited his fiftieth birthday with excitement and anticipation. Many a society hostess spent an anxious few weeks fretting over the arrival of an all-important invitation. Ironically, it was on the great day itself, right then and there, that it happened...The dutiful eulogies were about to be given by his most trusted lieutenants – one moment he was benignly acknowledging effusive greetings, awarding awaited kisses, exchanging ritual handshakes and embraces, indulging in predictable small-talk and in the next, he was engulfed in a choking cloud of despair. *In the midst of a perennial celebration of his life and achievements, at the zenith of his power and popularity, he was stricken with a sudden and inexplicable self-loathing.*

With effort, he maintained an outward calm and continued the endless round of buddying and glad-handing. The only thing that came to mind during the speeches was a similar event that he had attended for his one-time friend, Robert Maxwell. Was this the psychological vacuum that Maxwell had occupied before his final leap into the ocean from the stern of a liner? He began to shiver despite the warmth of the banqueting hall and the fulsomeness of the speeches.

To the surprise of all, he left for Monte Carlo the very next morning, telling his PA only that: "I will return when I return." There he remained for more than a month playing the tables each day until the small hours. Previous gambling had been no more than a diversion during extended stays at the world's premier hotels, but now he played like a man possessed: Lady Luck used codes: a winning night meant hope and possible redemption, a losing run kindled all fear and foreboding. When rubberneckers from the international set surrounded his table and ooh-ed and aah-ed at the alternating swings of his fortune, he swept them with a regard something akin to pity... the money was *irrelevant,* the stakes were far higher, he was playing the Fates.

He returned to London, as if from Lourdes, or from some high-altitude Himalayan ashram; re-energised and re-focused. Disregarding the management and executive hierarchy of his vast and complex empire, he began to make spirited interventions into its chain of command. Rows and resignations followed and sackings and severances. Eventually, even the City picked up on the rumours and began to whisper that Old Man Reed was losing his marbles. Corporate investors took fright and the group experienced its first ever bear run. Whilst there were always sycophants at the ready to pander to his daily interventions, he lost the support and loyalty of those members of the organisation whom he most respected. George had attempted to recapture the all-seeing, all-knowing, early monolithic glory days and had failed and now, all that he wanted, was to walk away from it all.

His enormous personal fortune would continue to accumulate unabated, but he was in an extremely dark place. Those that called upon him found him growing increasingly immune to the many diversions that his great wealth made possible. Soon a trickle of resignations began from the domestic staff of his Surrey farm. He chose to spend more time alone at the Park Lane penthouse... The housekeeper there, was the last to go − made weary by his latter-day rudeness and mood swings, the constant mess of left-over food, empty booze containers and broken furniture. George refused all counselling and became abusive when friends that remained pressed the case. Days and nights passed in a haze of drunken depression.

One mid-morning just before Christmas, as he surfaced to the customary hammering hangover, he discovered that he was not alone in his bed. A waif hardly out of childhood lay beside him, sleeping soundly. She smelled strongly of cheap Cologne and her heavy amateurish make-up had stained the bedcover. George leapt naked from the bed in shock.

She awoke and smiled. 'You couldn't manage anything last night, Mister, so I stayed on,' she told him. 'I'll have to charge you. If you're feeling better, I'll give you your money's-worth now?'

George stood there appalled, shocked and attempting to cover his modesty, as she tried again to interpret his mood.

'I knows of many that would 'ave just offed and nicked your wallet. I'm honest and what's more, I'm clean – no worries... But all that makes me more expensive.' To her amazement, George began to cry and to ask for her forgiveness. It was a response that lay outside the borders of her varied professional experience.

Half an hour later, replenished with coffee, she took her leave. He had paid her in full for nothing more than a good night's sleep. Diamond geezer... It was certainly something to tell the girls about – blimey, they'd be forming a queue!

George sat for a long time. He drank more coffee. He tried to focus on the events of the past months. The incident had put everything into sharp relief. It was a second watershed and silently he thanked her. He looked around himself at the sordid grotto that he now called home. *He was going to climb right out of it.* He stumbled over to the pile of unread newspapers in the hall and pulled the latest from the letterbox. It informed him that today was December the twenty-third – just a day away from Christmas. He churned through the bedside debris until he came upon his watch. It confirmed the date: Christmas... it used to be special.

Lady Fortune had given him an opportunity; perhaps, even a final chance? If he could just jet away, get himself together again... He would swim, take some sunshine, keep away from wine, women and song and try to re-think it all. Not Bondi, nor Hawaii, not Palm Springs nor the Copacabana. Somewhere lower key, where there was less chance of recognition: maybe South Africa or the Caribbean?

He rang *Far Range Travel* in Knightsbridge, gave his name and demanded that the clerk find him an instant luxury holiday – money no object, anywhere warm and quiet, no celebrity haunts, instant booking required.

It so happened, that the young clerk was one of a tiny handful of Londoners who had never heard of George Reed; to him, the request was sounding very much like a wind-up. He stalled a little, asked more questions.

'Just *do it* and get back to me,' said George, testily and rang off. Despite his inclinations towards a better self, he drew the line at having *anyone* query his instructions.

It had been a busy afternoon and the clerk decided against ringing back. Fifty minutes later, Mr Preston of *Far Range Travel* was demanding to know, *who* amongst his minions, had had the temerity to snub the all-powerful, George Reed!! After despatching the hapless clerk home to a jobless Christmas, Mr Preston personally arranged George's two weeks at the *Hotel Horatio Nelson*, Antigua – at the company's expense, of course.

At seven thirty on the evening of Christmas Eve, George stood outside his Park Lane penthouse beside a single exclusive Fendi designer suitcase. He hailed a cab parked up nearby. As he sank back into the rear seat and relaxed, he reminded himself that this was a new beginning: he would sleep away the flight and arrive to a cloudless blue sky.

'Going somewhere nice?' asked the cabbie, as he picked his way through Knightsbridge. George did not deign to reply. He pulled the collar of his Givenchy overcoat, close around his neck and glanced out at the scurryings of last minute, West End shoppers.

To George's surprise the driver took the Kensington Road turn. 'What's wrong with the A4 flyover?' he demanded, through the dividing glass.

'A bus has taken a wallop on the Cromwell Road,' said the cabbie. 'I heard it's bloody chaos down there, Mate.'

George reclined back into his seat as the cab weaved its way up Kensington High Street and crossed the junction with Holland Road. So far, it had taken less than ten minutes; barring problems on the M4, he would reach Heathrow with time to spare. They approached Olympia and inexplicably, the driver took a sudden sharp right and pulled up outside the main entrance.

'What the Devil's going on?' demanded George, 'I've a bloody plane to catch!'

'Sorry, Squire,' said the cabbie. 'Won't take a minute.'

As he spoke, the rear passenger doors were flung open and two muscular individuals piled in − one on each side of George. Quickly they linked an arm apiece through George's elbows, pinning him forcibly between them. The driver moved off in the direction of the Hammersmith fly-over, as if nothing had happened.

'What in hell-' yelled George, now beside himself with anger and shock.

'I'm Steve and that's Mick,' said the thug to his left. 'Now just pipe down old fella and no harm will come to you... I'm a nice enough geezer, but Mick can cut up very nasty.'

George's fury subsided to fear. 'This is no taxi!' he proclaimed.

A grin appeared on the face of the cabbie-who-was-not-a-cabbie. 'You're right about that,' he said.

'Let me out immediately!' shouted George.

The two men tightened their grips.

'So where you flying to from Heathrow?' enquired Steve.

'What the *hell*'s it to do with you?'

'We ask the questions.'

George began to struggle violently and to kick forward at the furniture behind the driver. Mick, produced a handgun and spoke for the first time.

'Do that again and I'll finish you right now.'

'Please,' said George, immediately subdued. 'What on earth d'you want with me?'

'That's better; much more friendly,' growled Mick.

'Relax,' said Steve. 'Just do as you're told and you'll come to no harm. We're what you might call *mobile highwaymen.* There's always rich pickings from around your way.' The man was actually grinning. 'What's your name, anyway? Let's try and keep this sociable.'

George ignored him and Mick returned the gun to his ribs.

'George,' he gasped, 'George Reed.'

Fortunately, the name seemed to mean nothing to the three men.

'Well you look like a fat cat, George,' said Steve. 'Designer luggage, Rolex watch, gold bracelet, beautiful overcoat-'

'Turn out your pockets,' demanded Mick.

George produced a fat wallet and his passport.

'Any good?' asked the driver.

'Jackpot,' said Steve. 'We'll have to haggle over the Rolex, but the guy's a gold mine.'

'First class to Antigua,' said Mick, as he counted the cash and traveller's cheques. 'I knew you was a fat cat.'

They had now reached the M4 and George was gripped by mounting panic.

'You've got everything,' he gasped. 'Can't you just drop me on the hard shoulder?'

Steve smiled. 'I told you to relax, George, and no harm will come to you... We're going to do a little u-turn at the next junction and take you back to where you can find the right cash machine. We want these golden bank cards of yours to start coughing.'

'And then?'

'And then we drop you off somewhere quiet. You'll have a bit of a walk home, that's all.' He saw the renewed fear in George's eyes. 'Play ball and you'll be fine. It's not as though you can't afford all of this, is it?'

George shivered involuntarily. 'Head for the Strand,' he said, 'that's where I bank.'

Mick removed the gun from his side. 'There we are, that's what we call cooperation, George.'

To the casual clubber or theatre-goer, it would have appeared that a couple of chaps had climbed out of a taxi to replenish their wallets, before a night on the town. Mick stood close up against George at the cash machine, with the gun concealed in a deep pocket. Steve lounged against the taxi door and the driver remained behind the wheel, ready to burn rubber at a moment's notice.

'Come on man, *again*...' hissed Mick, as he pocketed yet another bundle of notes. George emptied the limit on the remaining three cards before convincing his tormentor that there was no more to be had that night.

His mind was working furiously – *why couldn't the next guy in the queue be savvy enough to realise that something untoward was going on?* They walked back to the taxi. There had been no chance of escape and he was convinced that Mick would have used the weapon if need be.

'Well done,' said Steve, with a bright smile, as they climbed back into the taxi.

'That's me finished!' shouted George, 'You've got what you wanted, now let me go, you bastards.'

'Steady! Steady!' remonstrated Steve. 'All in good time, George! – Now be a good man and write down the PIN codes for those cards and hand them back over. I promise then, we won't be troubling you further.'

The taxi rolled on down the Strand, took a left to cross Waterloo Bridge and turned left again into Stamford Street to follow the river in the direction of Bermondsey. It was unfamiliar territory to George. At the end of Jamaica Road they entered Plough Way. His alarm bells were ringing again; where in hell were they taking him?

They pulled up quite suddenly and the driver jumped out. He was carrying a flash light.

'Come on, George; off we go,' said Steve. It sounded far from reassuring. He felt the cold steel of the pistol again in the back of his neck.

'Walk!' ordered Mick.

'Down here,' said the driver, as he led the way along several paths. George glimpsed shining water once or twice. They were in the Docklands. The driver came to a halt and his flashlight illuminated the door of what looked like a disused warehouse.

'Shall I finish him off?' demanded Mick. 'We could dump him in the dock?'

'We're not into murder,' replied the driver grimly. 'No need, the cold will do for him anyway... There'll be no one along here over Christmas. Dump him by the wall and chuck some of those cardboard cartons over him.'

Before George had time to react, he was dealt a vicious blow to the temple from the butt end of Mick's pistol. He collapsed like a de-stringed puppet.

'Shit! Blood all over my sleeve,' said Mick, as the three men walked back up the path.

'Mick...' said the driver reproachfully. 'You always have to go that one step further.'

George began to recover consciousness at around three in the morning. He had no way of knowing, as he was now without a watch. It was pitch dark and quite warm. He tried to raise himself but fell back immediately as the first wave of pain crossed his brain. He touched the pain centre on the left side of his head and was surprised to find that it seemed to be covered in some kind of dressing. The pad felt wet and sticky. A sudden rustling sound close by made him jump with fright. He was rewarded by a fresh onslaught of pain.

'Oh, so you're waking up are you?' said a small, frail voice.

'Whose that?' he demanded into the void. He thrashed out with an arm, almost as terrified as in the first few moments of his abduction.

'Steady! Steady!' chided the voice. 'You'll do us both harm!'

A small torch lamp flickered to life. His eyes adjusted painfully and he found himself face to face with a wizened old lady. She waved the lamp slowly backwards and forwards, carefully inspecting his wound. He took in the total squalor of their surroundings. He was lying beneath some sort of cardboard shelter and his body had been covered in all manner of assorted old coats and cotton waste.

'What the bloody hell?' he managed, before the roof began to spin and he was forced to lie back again.

'Now that was silly,' scolded the old crone, as she sucked noisily on her toothless gums. 'You'd best lie quiet there, my son.'

She fell into a violent coughing fit and pushed the lamp towards him. He watched trance-like, as she struggled to regain her breath. The effort was pushing beads of sweat through her grimy wrinkles.

'Now look what you've made me go and do,' she choked, as she took a bottle of blue liquid from beneath her covers. She swigged heavily and George smelled the unmistakeable fumes of methylated spirit. Her breathing quietened. 'Stops me cough and keeps me warm,' she confided, squinting at the bottle appreciatively.

George attempted again to rise onto his elbows.

'Look,' he groaned. 'Really, I have to get out of here.'

'You ain't going nowhere in this frost,' said the old lady, 'Darn near died out there, you did... and darn near killed me, pulling you into here.' She coughed again heavily and George saw blood in the corners of her mouth. 'This is my place and nobody else's. You can stay put till morning and then, good riddance.'

George tried desperately to remember what had happened to him, but his mind simply refused to engage... there was something about a holiday? Hadn't he been on his way somewhere?

The old girl's features softened somewhat. 'Here, eat this,' she said, as she pulled a wrapped sandwich from beneath the covers. 'It fell off the shelf in Marks and Sparks. You look like you could use a drink, as well?' She reached back into the covers and produced half a bottle of red wine. 'This is me best stuff,' she confided, 'I won't be giving you the meths, 'cause it can send you blind. Here. Cheers! It's Christmas morning. Eat and drink, it will please me.'

He ate the turkey and stuffing sandwich and drank gratefully from the bottle. The sandwiches tasted delicious and the wine was excellent. The old lady watched intently, her expression a mixture of pride and concern. 'Told you it was good stuff,' she said. 'Have all you want, I'm best with the meths and I ain't hungry.'

He passed back the bottle and thanked her, feeling guilty that it was perhaps the only food and drink that she possessed.

'You looks like a toff to me... Don't know what you did to deserve such a drubbing? Dumped you for dead, they did, but old Sarah heard 'em and came out looking.'

Everything came flooding back. Everything up to the point where they had crossed Waterloo Bridge. The bastards must have beaten him unconscious and left him in the cold and darkness. It was true, this old lady had more than likely saved his life.

'Listen – I'm so grateful. It's all coming back to me. I was mugged. I have to go for help. Get to the police.' The effort of speech and the small amount of wine had sent his head spinning again.

The old lady was caught by another violent bout of coughing. She propped herself on one elbow and repeated the methylated cure. When she lay back she was clearly exhausted by her efforts. Her lips and jaw were in slight spasm, working backwards and forwards. She brushed a dank ringlet of hair from her forehead and gave him a long searching look. He saw that her eyes were dark brown and remarkably steady and unblinking.

'We're deep in the docklands,' she informed him. 'It's dangerous out there in the frost and the dark, you could fall off a pier-head, down into the water.'

He realised with some dismay that she was right. He was in no condition to stumble around in the dark in a freezing, unlit, hazardous area. Here, at least it was warm and comfortable and as he had been patched up after a fashion, it made more sense to wait until first light.

'Maybe I'll try and get a little sleep then,' he told her. 'Thank you for what you have done.'

She looked pleased. 'You can call me Sarah Jones, Son,' she said. 'Everybody else does. I don't remember me proper name.' She took a final pull on the meths bottle.

'That stuff will kill you,' he told her.

She smiled a toothless smile, then lay back with her head only inches from his own. 'The Good Lord wanted me to celebrate Christmas... And besides,' she added shyly, 'I've never had a guest to share it with before.'

He closed his eyes and knew nothing until he became aware of shafts of sunlight illuminating the corners of the cardboard roof. He thought for a second that he was experiencing one of his familiar hangovers, but then touched the wound on his head and remembered.

There was a hand holding his own and it felt comforting. He lay for some moments doing nothing to release the grip. Beside him lay the strange old lady who had befriended him and saved him from freezing, or bleeding to death. She was lying on her back with her lips slightly parted, looking strangely serene and secure. It took a while longer for him to realise that she had died peacefully in her sleep.

When someone as wealthy and well-known as George Reed simply disappears, it catches the attention of the news hounds and the imagination of the general public. Only a tiny handful of George's most trusted financial and legal confidantes ever got to know of his whereabouts and they were paid handsomely to keep things that way.

Along the pavements, in the shop doorways, under the railway arches and across the docklands of South London, the bush telegraph was buzzing. A new charity had opened in Deptford: *The Sarah Jones Bed and Breakfast Hotel.* It catered exclusively for what it called: "the sons and daughters of the open road". A second place was due to open in Bermondsey and two more were planned for Southwark and Wapping.

According to its first guests, the SJ-B&BH was certainly more hotel than hostel. The manager had no truck with booze or drugs, although the notable exception was Christmas morning, when each guest was entitled to a free half-bottle of red wine.

You were waited on hand and foot at the *Sarah Jones,* people said.

Many of the regulars had known the real Sarah Jones.

'It's amazing,' said one old sweat to the manager. 'The brass that old girl must have had, yet she lived rough alongside us for all those years.'

Everybody said that he was all right, was the manager... His name was George. He was a bit of a toff, but he was all right, was George.

11

Mummy's Christmas Present

It was Christmas Eve morning. During the night it had snowed heavily and a late frost had added an icing-sugar sparkle to the virgin-white covering. When Kate and Samantha Darling opened their bedroom curtains they were amazed to see that the drab high street had been transformed into a white wonderland. The early morning traffic was slithering and sliding about and Mrs Edwards, from the floor below, was finding it difficult to cross from the flats to the bus stop. Suddenly the poor woman waved an arm in the air like a helicopter blade and fell flat on her bum in the snow. Kate and Sammy collapsed back on their beds in fits of giggles, then peeped out again, filled with the irrational fear that perhaps she had seen them, high up in their flat.

Little Sammy could hardly contain her excitement. During the past three of her five years, Birmingham had been snowless and therefore she had experienced white worlds only through the medium of Christmas cards and Disney films. She placed her tongue now on the residue of frost on the inside of the window pane and made a succession of semi-circular prints.

'Please can we go to the park? Please can we go to the park and make a snowman, Katie?' she begged.

'Don't *do* that − your tongue will stick to the glass and the firemen will have to come and cut it off,' scolded Kate.

Big sisters knew about stuff like that and Sammy gave her a look of concern. 'Can it be sticked on again?' she asked.

Kate treated the question with all the lofty contempt of her additional seven years. 'Come on, hurry up and dress, we have to be ready to meet Daddy in town to buy Mummy's present.'

'But it's all snowy... Can't we go to the park instead?' Sammy insisted.

'Maybe Daddy will let us, when we come back from town,' said Kate.

Sammy made no attempt to hide her disappointment, she stomped off to the bathroom and closed the door with a big bang. The black plastic toilet seat was always sliding sideways and her bottom came into sudden contact with the freezing cold of the ceramic bowl. This made her even more angry. Now she tried practising her *very worst scowl* in the cracked mirror opposite. It was a good one − most of her chin had disappeared under the bottom lip and both eyes looked very, very scary indeed. She would try to remember how it was done when she went back out to Katie. First she would concentrate on the job in hand and watch her cheeks go red with the effort − they always did. Why was that, she wondered?

Katie was knocking on the door and shouting for her to hurry up... It was time to be quiet as a mouse. She had been looking forward to buying Mummy's present, but that had been before she knew about the snowfall. Never mind, perhaps it would be fun catching the bus into Birmingham? Maybe it would slip and slide and bang into things, like at the fair? That would good! Her mood was brightening and as she washed her hands and face, she caught her reflection and was surprised to see that she was actually smiling. That would *never* do — Katie would see that her mood had changed. She practised the scowl again — not bad!

'Daddy says you're to open this door right now and never to lock it again!' shouted her big sister angrily, from the outside.

'Coming...,' trilled Samantha, as sweetly as she could; but already, she had decided to count slowly to thirty, just to make Katie really mad!

'Bye then girls!' shouted Daddy from the doorway. 'You're clear on everything then, Katie?'

'Yes, Dad!' called Kate. 'See you outside the town hall!'

'OK then, bye girls! Take care. I'll give your love to Mummy — you can visit her tomorrow.'

'Bye, Dad!' they chorused from the breakfast table. They had finished their cornflakes and Kate was operating the toaster. It was not that either of them particularly liked toast, but more because Kate had been given permission to operate the toaster. She had grown up quickly since their mother's illness. Sammy watched her enviously and wished with all of her heart that soon, she too could be grown up enough to operate the toaster.

As soon as they had eaten they did the washing up together and then began to put on their outdoor clothes.

'Can you help me with my buttons?' asked Samantha, reluctantly. 'They're always too hard.'

Katie stretched the material across her sister's chest until the toggles on the duffel coat finally pushed through. They were both in need of new winter coats. Daddy said that they must have shrunk, but Kate knew he hadn't the money to buy new ones since he lost his job. He said he was going to take the coats to *Marks and Spencer* and get the money back. He was always saying things like that... but the coats were very old and worn, and she knew that he never would.

'It smells of wee,' said Samantha, as the lift scraped its way down from the twenty-first floor.

'It's because it's Saturday,' said Kate, authoritatively. 'Mum says the men can't hold their beer on Friday nights and the caretaker's not there with his mop on Saturdays.'

As they made their way out of the double doors in the foyer of the flats, the wind howled, as it always did, around the base of the building and the penetrating cold hit them head on.

'You have to breathe in little bits at a time,' said Katie, 'otherwise your lungs can freeze right up.'

'Can they?' asked Sammy fearfully. She practised small intakes, but was quickly out of breath and hoped that Katie wouldn't notice the larger gulps that she was obliged to take.

'Sometimes, it can be so cold that you have to catch your words in your hands and take them inside to thaw out, before anyone can hear what you've said,' said Kate.

Samantha was mightily impressed by that.

They crossed from the flats towards the main road and as soon as Sammy hit the snow she forgot all about the dire frozen-lung warnings and began to jump in and out of the drifts, defacing as much of its pristine surface as possible. Kate tried her best to cling to her twelve-years of maturity but quickly succumbed. Soon they were diving and jumping, rolling and sliding and throwing huge armfuls of snow over one another. By pure luck, Kate noticed the number 22 city centre bus arriving and they ran red-faced, panting and joyful to the bus stop, to catch it in the nick of time

.

The top end of New Street was filled with the sound of carols blasting from a row of speakers strung across two buildings. Father Christmas was about to begin his journey through the town and an excited crowd milled around the town hall, anxious to catch a glimpse. Kate began to pull Sammy through to a vantage point and good-hearted adults allowed them passage. Sammy thought that Father Christmas looked magnificent, sitting up there on his huge sleigh with his six reindeer in attendance. It was puzzling – she felt sure that she could hear the sound of a car engine coming from somewhere beneath the sleigh.

She pointed to the gold writing on the huge red ribbon bedecking the reindeer. 'What does it say, Katie?' she asked.

'It says: *Friends of Selly Oak Hospital.*'

'Mummy's in a hospital,' said Sammy.

'She's in a hospice,' Kate replied.

Santa moved off slowly in the direction of the Bull Ring and Kate looked at her wrist watch with the forty jewels. Daddy had said that they were real, but some had fallen out and he had stuck them back with glue. It was almost half past eleven and the large square near the town hall was alive with the hustle and bustle of Christmas shoppers.... time to think about Mummy's Christmas present.

Sammy could see that there was something terribly, terribly wrong. Kate had been looking in her purse and now she was checking all of her pockets over and over again.

'I can't find our money for Mummy's present,' she said, very near to tears. 'Maybe I lost it, playing in the snow?'

'Oh, Katie... Do you think it felled out?'

'Did *you* have it? demanded Kate. 'Did you pick it up from the table after breakfast?'

'No, no, Katie... I didn't see it!' cried poor Sammy. The thrust of her sister's accusation had made her feel needlessly guilty and she began to weep.

'Oh... Oh... Oh... what can we do? What can we do?' cried Kate. 'We've lost our Christmas money for Mummy's present!' She began to wail so loudly that Sammy found room in her own distress to put a protective arm around her.

A kindly gentleman paused to look at the two distressed little girls and a lady passing by with two children no older than Samantha, stopped beside him.

'What's the matter, Luvvie?' asked the man.

The children were too distressed to reply.

'There, there, Sweetheart,' said the lady. 'Whatever is the matter?'

More people began to pause beside the little group.

'Are they all right?' asked an elderly lady.

'I just found them like this,' said the kind gentleman.

'We've lost- we've lost-' stammered Kate.

'You've lost your mummy?' asked the lady.

'No...n-n-n...no,' sobbed Kate.

'Mummy's at the hospice,' wailed Sammy.

An audible sigh ran through the growing crowd that had now formed a small circle around the girls.

The kindly gentleman tried again. 'Come on, Dear; try to tell us, what has happened?'

'We've lost all of our money,' cried Sammy.

'It was for Mummy's Christmas present,' sobbed Kate, 'and we don't know where it is.'

'Katie put it in her pocket and now it's gone,' added Sammy.

'Oh, dear, dear...' said the kindly gentleman. 'Well how much money did you lose, girls, can you remember?'

'It was nearly four pounds,' whispered Kate.

'Well perhaps I can help out a little?' said the kindly gentleman. He removed his trilby hat and placed a ten-shilling note in it.

The first lady smiled and took out her purse. 'And there's a pound from me,' she said.

Some of the people reached into their pockets and purses and others drifted quickly away. A gent dressed smartly in a camel-hair overcoat, took out his wallet and added two one pound notes. Other shoppers pitched in with shillings, sixpences, three penny bits, florins and half-crowns. Soon the hat was half-full with donations from the kindly crowd. One lady on the perimeter pushed forward with a five pound note and took four pounds back in change.

'Well, well, well...' said the kindly gentleman, as he emptied out the notes and coins and handed them over to the two young girls. 'That should go a long way towards putting things right, don't you think?'

'And when you see your mummy, you be sure to tell her that you love her, and have a very happy Christmas,' said the first lady, with tears of her own.

The onlookers smiled and one or two others were also wet-eyed. The kindly gentleman retrieved his hat and to some applause, ruffled little Sammy's hair. The crowd began to disperse, with everyone feeling happy to have participated in such a spontaneous gesture of seasonal goodwill.

Kate and Samantha walked over to the Council House and sat down on the steps.

'It's lots and lots,' said Sammy. 'Is it more than we lost, Katie? Is it?'

'Lots and lots more,' said Kate. 'Let's see.'

Kate began to count the money into Sammy's lap. First the notes and then the coins. By the time she had finished they found that they had a total of seventeen pounds, twelve shillings and nine pence. It was more money than either of them had ever seen before. Kate put it carefully into her deepest pocket.

'Come on, Sammy!' she cried joyfully. 'We have to meet Daddy down in the Bull Ring in twenty minutes!'

Samantha followed her elder sister along New Street, past the Odeon Cinema and down the steps towards the Bull Ring market. 'Katie,' she asked. 'Why does Daddy want us to pretend that we don't know who he is?'

'It's just a Christmas game,' said Kate.

'It was a good job he came and spoke to everyone, just when you'd lost the money,' said Sam.

Kate nodded vigorously.

'It really was, wasn't it!' She tapped the pocket in her old coat and turned to Samantha with a worried look.

'Oh, oh... Sammy, Sammy! I think that I must have a hole in my pocket... and I've lost the money, all over again!'

12

Her First Christmas

For many years, Dan had told no one of the relationship and even now, only a handful of his closest friends knew anything about her. It had been a long, long time to have known someone so well and yet never to have met up with them. All of that was about to change. Soon he would be on his way to Helsinki and it would be love at first sight − of that he was sure. *Love at first sight* − he chuckled at his weird frame of mind. God knows, there was love enough already! She had been always in his thoughts, since the first he had known of her. Throughout the long years of waiting, he had yearned for her, pined for her, dreamt of little else other than the day when he would finally meet up with her, in the flesh.

He replayed the phone call over in his mind: Could he make it over before Christmas? Would it be convenient? *Would it be convenient!* − For her, he would have paddled to Helsinki by canoe. The timing could not have been better; first there would be the opportunity to be alone with her for the first few precious days. Afterwards, she would come and spend her first ever Christmas in England, with all of the excitement of finally meeting and greeting his numerous friends.

He hoped that his reply had sounded sufficiently cool and assured, but somehow, he doubted it – "Yes, just firm up on the actual date and I'll make arrangements to take off the necessary time from work," – he *thought* he remembered saying... but his head had been in too much of a swim to be certain.

Despite his anticipation and enthusiasm, it was natural, he supposed, that he still harboured a few worries and doubts: He had not been himself for some time – as the frequent trips to his GP confirmed. The final days of waiting were playing out like an eternity and he found himself constantly reappraising her: physically, she looked a stunner: tall and slim with long shapely legs, hazel eyes, dark hair, nice smile and beautiful teeth; *very* much to his taste. She was intelligent too and packed a wicked sense of humour. All mighty fine, but none of it really got down to the *bedrock* of his worries... The key issue was: *would she fit in?* His friends and his easy-going bachelor lifestyle were precious to him. Within that scenario, would it work, or would she feel out of place and gradually become isolated and withdrawn? He knew that he would do all in his power to make it right for her, but in the final analysis, there could be no guarantees.

For the first evening in a long time, he missed a trip to his local watering hole, *The Firs*, and sat drinking at home, with his fingers wrapped far too tightly around the whiskey bottle. He was pleased that the drink was having a therapeutic effect – it could have wound him up the other way. Stupid, stupid paranoia! The friends who *knew,* referred to her in conversation as if they'd met her already. What greater vote of confidence could there be than that? He could be sure that they would do their loyal best to welcome her.

The weekend before his Monday departure finally crept around. He used the Saturday morning to shop for Christmas presents. He fully intended to spoil her and set about buying her an entire wardrobe of clothes. Helsinki would be well below zero − but no need to go *too* heavy on arctic kit − she would be making her new home in London. It was fun choosing. He picked up a few strange looks in the underwear section, but hell − for the first time in his life, he had the job of making a woman happy.

If all went to plan, he would be in Helsinki for five days. Back to London, in time for Christmas Eve at *The Firs;* it was always the biggest night of the year. Friends would be there in numbers, there would be music, the champagne would flow and he hoped that she would have no problems with being the centre of attention. His heart was in overdrive. "Relax!" he told himself... Stupid to fantasise in advance; she would be her own woman and would want to make her mark in her own way − not necessarily in the manner that his ego was deciding that she might want. Time would tell. He had to take it all more calmly.

By Sunday evening he felt a little more grounded and arranged to meet a few friends for a quiet drink. They wished him luck and God speed and then it was back to the flat and early to bed.

He checked over passport, money and took a final look at his packing. He was taking virtually nothing for himself; all of his thoughts were centred upon her welfare. It was vital to provide her with the best possible experience for her first encounter with the country that he loved.

The flight was smooth and uneventful. At the airport exit he read out the unpronounceable address to a taxi driver and the man gave him a blank look.

'Here, see for yourself,' he offered.

'Ah!' said the driver, as recognition dawned. He uttered something utterly incomprehensible, that must have mirrored the writing on the card, and set about dumping Dan's luggage into the boot.

'Some language, Finnish,' said Dan with a smile, as he climbed into the passenger seat. The driver smiled back uncomprehendingly and offered a further unintelligible sentence of his own. The adventure had begun! They were crossing the beautiful city of Helsinki.

'Mr Miller, isn't it?' enquired the girl at Reception. Clearly, he was expected and this made Dan feel much more relaxed.

'It is,' he replied, as he paid off his driver.

'I'll get someone to show you through to your private suite,' said the girl.

Mr Virtanen came by at four o'clock. 'Good trip, Daniel?' he asked, as he extended a hand.

'Fine, fine,' replied Dan, nervously.

'Well – this is the big one.'

Dan flashed a grateful smile – for, without the constant encouragement and reassurance of Mr Virtanen, he would never have seen things through.

'And I hear that you're to be called Danielle? – Excellent choice, excellent choice. You won't have to go through all of that tiresome business of changing bank cards, etc.'

'That was a consideration, Mr Virtanen, but more importantly, I like the name. It still leaves plenty to change: passport, driving licence, social security details, etc. etc.'

'Excellent! Good...good...good,' said Mr Virtanen, absently. 'Well, see you in theatre at nine in the morning, so try to get a good night's sleep.'

'Thank, you Mr Virtanen, I'll do my best.'

'With any luck, you should be saying hello to Danielle, at about five thirty, tomorrow afternoon; though of course, you shouldn't expect to feel at your feminine best for a few days.'

'That's a small price to pay, Mr Virtanen,' said Dan appreciatively.

'It will be her *first* Christmas and that means all the world to me.'

13
A Dog for Christmas

'No more "if's" and "buts", I'm telling you, I want a puppy for Christmas and that's *final!'* shouted Stella. She was fed up with the haggling, the evasiveness and the prevarication and fast coming to the end of her tether. *Surely to God* it wasn't that much to ask?

Mike was miles away, sitting in front of his screen, attempting to hide his impatience, trying to look and sound sympathetic. He noted the renewed determination on her face. *Had she any real idea of just how difficult it was going to be to organise?* He groaned inwardly at this latest manifestation of his wife's fast-growing paranoia. She was lonely he knew, but given the distance between them, just how much did she imagine that he could do about it? – Really, it was just too bad! She'd known the score from the beginning, when the job first came up.

He tried again.

'Come on now, Stella,' he soothed. 'How in Heaven's name are you going to be able to look after the needs of a young puppy?'

'Don't you dare start on that one again, Mike! It's more than enough that I'm stuck here without you.

115

Have you any idea what it's like — cooped up twenty-four-seven, trying to cope all alone with Harry and Tina? *You're* all right... at least you can leave the job behind at the end of the day; take off and go for a drink and a meal somewhere. I'm fraying at the edges, they're getting on my nerves. I don't want to end up doing something impulsive or stupid... an animal would really help to keep me sane.'

'But it's not as if it's forever, Honey,' he wheedled. 'We'll be back together real soon.'

'If you love me, you'll find a way. I want a dog, Mike and that's it.'

Mike slammed his hands on the desk in frustration.

'Be *reasonable*, Stella! How in hell am I going to organise it? Damn it, I'm down here in Florida. It's not as though we're talking to each other from just around the corner!'

He could hear the sound of the sobbing through the earpiece and knew that there was no alternative but to modify his tone. 'Oh, *come on,* Love... As soon as we get back together, I promise, the first thing I'll do, is to go out and buy a dog.'

'You're not listening. If you really cared about me, distance wouldn't matter. You'd send one to the moon and back.'

'Stella, that's so unreasonable, just *think* what you're saying.'

'It's a woman's prerogative.'

'Think of the *mess* Honey, think of the expense and where would you exercise it? I'm not even sure that you've enough time to look after it.'

Stella was not to be dissuaded.

'You know darned well − I have *all the time in the world*. I never go *anywhere*. It's the same boring routine every day, with Harry and Tina. I just go round and around in circles. You've no idea how many hours a day I spend staring out of the window, thinking of you? Mike, I've had it; I'm totally spaced out.'

'Just try to hold on, Baby. It won't be for long, it will soon go by.'

'If you *patronise* me one more time, I swear I'll totally lose it! You still don't get it, do you? − I accept that we can't be together... so the least you can do is to indulge me. I'm not going to say it again: Mike: *I want a dog for Christmas!'*

Mike was almost out of ideas. He played the one hand he'd kept in reserve.

'Think Darling... We know Harry's really scared of dogs; just how's that one going to figure?'

'He says he doesn't mind.'

'He *said* that?'

'More or less, that's what he said... And Tina's keen now − at first she was worried for her pink rats, but now she thinks it could be OK.'

Mike took one last shot:

'It's a crazy idea − there'll be dog hair floating around, doggy-do, saliva and God knows what else.'

Stella broke.

'To hell with you, Mike! You get me a dog organised right now, or I *wreck* this place! I promise, that'll be last you'll ever see or hear of me, or Harry, or Tina!'

Mike replaced the phone at *Mission Control* in the Kennedy Space Centre and turned apologetically to the Chief.
'Sorry, Steve. I gave it my best shot.'
'It's a bummer, Mike', said Steve. 'Clearly, she's become unstable out there. We have to take her threat seriously; the lives of all three of them have become increasingly at risk.
Mike nodded unhappily.
'Best get yourself on-line to a pet shop and find some gift-wrap too. The knock-on effects of this are incalculable... to accommodate a pooch, we'll have to reschedule the entire contents of the next Shuttle Payload,' said Steve.

He made a mental note to arrange a follow-up with the mission psych': the time had come to add an *Animal Lovers* section, to NASA's screening tests.

I hope that you enjoyed these short stories. If you did, I have one favour to ask of you - your rating or review on my Amazon site would make my day!

You may also wish to try my published novels: *Circuit* (2017) and *Beyond the Sad-faced Clown* (2018). They are available, under the author's name, from the publisher, Austin Macauley and from Amazon Books, Smashwords.com and all major UK book retail outlets.

Happy reading!!

Keith Bullock.

Printed in Great Britain
by Amazon

33272209R00070